THE BOOK OF
RIGA

EDITED BY EVA EGLĀJA-KRISTSONE
& BECCA PARKINSON

First published in Great Britain in 2018 by Comma Press
commapress.co.uk

'The Birds of Ķīpsala Island' was first published in Latvian in *Ķīpsalas putni* (Dienas Grāmata, 2009). 'The Night Shift' was first published in *Trakie veči* (Dienas Grāmata, 2016). 'The Hare's Declaration' was first published in *Atgriešanās Itakā* (Dienas Grāmata, 2011). 'The Shakes' was first published in *Pilsētas šamaņi* (Dienas Grāmata, 2016). 'Westside Garden' was first published in *Septiņi stāsti par mīlu* (Literatūra un Māksla, 1992). 'Killing Mrs Cecilia Bochs' was first published in *Gardo vistiņu nedēļa* (Zvaigzne ABC, 2012). 'Where I Am' was first published in *Mēs. XX gadsimts* (Dienas Grāmata, 2011). 'A White Jacket with Gold Buttons' was first published in *Satori* (2014). 'Wonderful New Latvia' was first published in *Stāsti. Prozas lasījumi klātienē un neklātienē* (Dienas Grāmata, 2008). 'The Girl Who Cut My Hair' was first published in *Meitene, kas nogrieza man matus* (Mansards, 2011).

A CIP catalogue record of this book is available from the British Library.
ISBN: 1910974382
ISBN-13: 9781910974384

This book is published with the support of the Ministry of Culture of the Republic of Latvia and The Latvian Writers' Union.

Kultūras ministrija

The publisher gratefully acknowledges assistance from Arts Council England.

Printed and bound in England by Clays.

Contents

Foreword

Vaira Vīķe-Freiberga

THERE IS A LEGEND about Riga, which states that every hundred years a diminutive, mythical creature rises up out of the depths of the River Daugava and asks the first inhabitant he encounters: 'Is Riga complete?' If the answer is 'No, it's not finished', then the creature will disappear and Riga will be left to continue growing and prospering for another century. Should the day arise when an inhabitant of Riga answers, 'Yes, Riga is complete', then the whole city will disappear, engulfed by the waters, along with the mythical creature.

The official date of the founding of Riga, now the capital of Latvia, is 1201 – long before the birth of the Republic of Latvia only a century ago. This year, 2018, has been devoted to events and projects, both large and small, in honour of the Declaration of Independence on 18 November 1918. Even though half of the last century was spent under Soviet occupation, there is plenty to celebrate, recalling the accomplishments of the 20 years of independence between the two World Wars, and the 27 years that have elapsed since the renewal of independence in 1991. The one thing that Latvians must remember during these celebrations is not to say that the task of building our country is complete. It is a work in progress and will require the best efforts of each successive generation, in order to build upon and improve that which has gone before.

While Riga has been spared the symbolic waters of forgetfulness that the old legend warns about, it has not been spared the fires of war, with their bloodbaths and devastation, nor the scythe of the Grim Reaper during repeated bouts of the Black Death. After each period of growth in population, wealth and influence, there have been dark periods when there were just enough survivors left in the city to bury the mounds of corpses.

Riga was founded by Bishop Albert in 1201 near the mouth of the Daugava River (temporarily rechristened by the Germans as the 'Düna'), on the site of an ancient Liv[1] fishing village and minor trading post. Deep in the Bay of Riga, it provided a natural harbour, which remained ice-free even in winter. Already by the middle of the twelfth century, Hanseatic traders from the city of Lübeck had established a trading post at the same site. Long before that, well-established North-South trade routes for amber, furs, wax, and honey had been travelled ever since Roman times.

In 1199, just two years before the founding of Riga, Pope Innocent III issued a papal bull, or decree, declaring that a crusade against the last pagans in Europe would bring just as much merit to its participants as the crusades in the Holy Land, or the crusades against those denounced as heretics, like the Albigenses in the south of France. Knights from all parts of Western Europe answered the call, those from the German-speaking lands being the most numerous among them, and the most anxious to conquer new territories not that far from their homes. The Teutonic Order started their invasion in East Prussia and what is now Lithuania. Further north, in the territories of present-day Latvia and Estonia, the Order of the Livonian Brothers of the Sword engaged in a long century of bitter fighting before the territories of present-day Latvia were subjugated and, at least nominally, Christianised.

The period between the ninth and the eleventh centuries had seen a flowering of the peoples speaking languages of the

Baltic branch of the Indo-European language tree, and their territories extended from the Elbe in the West to the whole of what became Belarus in the East, although they lacked anything resembling political unity. The kings of local tribes fought the Vikings, and as well as each other, they fought the Finnic Livs and Estonians to the north, the Slavic tribes from the east, and the Germanic tribes from the south-west. They fought valiantly, but the territories they controlled kept shrinking. By the end of the thirteenth century, the Semigallians of south-central Latvia lost their last wooden castle of Sidrabene, after which their king Nameys (or Nameisis) led 100,000 of them south into exile to Lithuania, never to be heard from in the historical records again.

The early centuries of Riga were not dissimilar to the Latvian folk tales in which something was built in the daytime, only to be destroyed by the devil during the dark of the night. Through all of these major upheavals, however, the city kept growing, and traders, merchants and seafarers from many lands made the place their home. As a prosperous German-speaking city of increasing wealth and influence, it became a major player in the Hanseatic League,[2] operating under the rules of the city of Lübeck. The Old Town of Riga, now a UNESCO World Heritage Site, has kept traces of that period in buildings dating back to the Middle Ages, and in the narrow, winding streets that still bear the names of ancient guilds, such as Weavers' Street or Smiths' Street. The red-brick Dome Cathedral[3] is a close cousin of similar churches all across Northern Europe, and slender church spires have been defining the iconic skyline of Riga for centuries, just as the famed seven golden spires define Lübeck's. Riga converted to Lutheranism soon after the Reformation, but in due time came to host Catholic and Orthodox churches, as well as synagogues.

Just like elsewhere in Northern Europe, the burghers of Riga fought fiercely to preserve as much independence as possible. By 1221 they had acquired the right to self-administration, independent of church authority. Between 1561 and 1582, Riga was an empire-free city, then came under the Polish-Lithuanian Commonwealth for the next half century. For almost a century – between 1629 and 1721 – Riga was the largest, and later the second-largest Swedish city after Stockholm, but was incorporated into the Russian Empire from 1721 (the treaty of Nystad after the Great Northern War) until the Revolution of 1917. It became the capital of the independent Republic of Latvia in 1918, but came under both Soviet and Nazi occupations during the Second World War. Riga was styled as the capital of Soviet Socialist Republic of Latvia until August 1991, but regained its status as the capital of independent Latvia after the dissolution of the Soviet Union.

The earliest writings mentioning Riga were medieval chronicles about the Christian conquest, written in Latin, much like later travel accounts of visitors from southern lands. These were succeeded by publications in German and the establishment of German publishers in the city, like the one which published Immanuel Kant's *Critique of Pure Reason*, even though Kant was teaching at Königsberg. It was also upon Kant's recommendation that Wolfgang Gottfried Herder arrived in Riga on 1 December 1764, to take up a post as teacher at the Riga Dome School. Not surprisingly, the stolid burghers of Riga fired him five years later, finding his romantic ideals too liberal for their taste. Non-religious literature in the local Latvian language remained scant until an explosion of it in the second half of the nineteenth century, linked to the movement known as the First Latvian National Awakening. A policy of intensive Russianisation was not introduced until the very end of the nineteenth century, and lasted only until the 1917 Revolution. Nevertheless, the result of it all was that most inhabitants of

Riga had to be bilingual at the very least, and frequently even trilingual or quadrilingual.

Now, as we mark the centenary of the Latvian Republic, Riga remains a multi-ethnic, multilingual city, with Latvian as the official language, but also a substantial Russian-speaking population, made up of ethnic Russians as well as a number of other nationalities from the former Soviet Union. Its demographic profile was drastically altered by Hitler's recall of all Baltic-Germans in 1938, a result of the secret protocol of his agreement with Stalin (known as the Molotov-Ribbentrop pact). The vibrant Jewish community was almost totally exterminated during the Nazi occupation, while the Latvian population was drastically reduced by repeated mass deportations to Siberia between 1940 and 1949, under Stalin's orders, as well as by a massive flight of refugees to the West at the very end of the Second World War. Today, next to Latvian, English has taken over as the lingua franca of the city, something of an irony at a time when the UK has voted to exit the European Union.

Ever since the Reformation introduced the idea that literacy was an essential prerequisite if every Christian was to read the Bible, the Protestant parts of Latvia have been literate, which means that they became increasingly informed about events elsewhere in Europe, especially during the French Revolution. The preaching of the Moravian Brothers in Vidzeme (the North-Central part of Latvia) strengthened the self-confidence of the oppressed Latvian peasants and encouraged them to organise, interact and pursue education. As serfdom was abolished at various stages throughout the 19th Century, Latvians started a mass movement seeking better and better education, acquiring property and relocating to the cities, Riga foremost among them. Riga started appearing as a vital presence in Latvian novels, short stories and poetry, and continues to do so to this day. It has become a major hub for air transportation and a magnet for a rapidly growing number of tourists. As a city, Riga also offers an extraordinary breadth of cultural events, boasts the most lively nightlife in all the Baltics, and has become a Mecca for admirers of either ornate Jugendstil (Art-Nouveau), wooden architecture, or both. Translations of literary works about Riga are a welcome development at this time, when European citizens still have a lot to learn about each other.

Vaira Vīķe-Freiberga
President of the Republic of Latvia, 1999-2007

Notes

1. Livs or Livonians: a Finnic ethnic group indigenous to northern Latvia and southwestern Estonia. The last person to have learned and spoken Livonian as a mother tongue, died in 2013, making Livonian extinct.
2. Hanseatic League: a commercial and defensive confederation of merchant guilds and their market towns. Growing from a few North German towns in the late 1100s, the League came to dominate Baltic maritime trade for three centuries along the coast of Northern Europe.
3. Riga Cathedral is commonly called the Dome Cathedral, a tautology as the word 'Dome' comes from the German, *dom*, meaning 'cathedral'.

Introduction

RIGA IS A CITY OF LEGENDS, myths and stories. Take, for instance, the story of Great Kristaps, passed down from one generation to the next, and retold in many different ways. According to one version, once upon a time, on the bank of the River Daugava, there lived a very strong man who made his living carrying people across the river on his back. One night a little boy approached him and asked him to carry him over. Although the weather was stormy, the man picked up the child and began carrying him across the river. With each step, the man found that the child was becoming heavier until by midstream only with the greatest of effort could he make it to shore. They say that Kristaps was rewarded with a heap of money that he used to buy all of Riga. At that time, the town was so small a wolf could run through it without being disturbed. Since then the city of Riga has grown rapidly, and likewise the stories about it and its people will never cease to spread.

The Daugava River is the line that divides Riga between the old stone spires and busy city centre on the right bank, and the creaking wooden houses and new glass towers on the left bank. The symbolism of the Daugava in the history of Riga and Latvia is so important it is known as the River of Destiny and Mother Daugava. Both banks are marked by five bridges, historical places, and objects, which feature prominently in the stories that follow, where they offer a physical and spiritual mapping of the city. The heart and soul of Latvia's capital city is Old Riga, where there are magnificent sights, historical landmarks and ancient architecture to see.

What is interesting though is that those stories set in Old Riga do not reflect the image of the city offered in tourist brochures, which paint the city with a particular atmosphere of romanticism and fascinating Hanseatic, Art Deco architecture. At the core of many of the stories featured in this anthology is an individual and social outrage. Prose writer Juris Zvirgzdiņš, in his story 'The Hare's Declaration', presents Old Riga as a place of action – a man who's lost his job decides to end his life conspicuously. He wanders through Riga looking for the right spot and, in the end, chooses the tower of St. Peter's Church, so as to be closer to the golden rooster weathervane and to God. St. Peter's Church is Riga's tallest church with a tower offering a breathtaking view of the red roofs of the Old Town, as well as the more modern part of the city, Riga Bay and the Daugava River, with its large port. From the bell tower of St. Peter's Church, a popular Latvian folksong 'Riga dimd' ('Riga resounds') is played five times a day:

Riga resounds, Riga resounds
Who made Riga so resound?

Not far from this Church is Riga Castle, which is the current workplace of the President of Latvia. After being freed from the Soviet yoke and gaining independence, Latvia became a part of the European Union; international investors and entrepreneurs moved to the city, transforming this part of Riga into a bustling metropolis. Sven Kuzmins' story 'The Shakes' gives an insight into the mind of a Swedish businessman, Jenson, who has a Latvian secretary working in his office in Old Riga. One day Jenson wants to share with his secretary an interesting and regular occurrence he has observed. Initially she doesn't see anything out of the ordinary in what he shows her – just cobbled pavement, shops, restaurants, the Castle Square. But then a small group appears shouting slogans and waving placards in the direction of the Castle; the people are calling for change.

The centre of Riga is no less beautiful than the Old Town, although it is a city centre of contrasts and underlying tension. Brīvības Iela or 'Freedom Street' is Riga's main thoroughfare; in different historical periods it was named after the Russian Tsar Alexander II, Lenin, and once even named after Hitler. Andra Neiburga's story takes the form of a flashback from the beginning of the twentieth century when, just a short distance from the Esplanade and the Nativity of Christ Orthodox Cathedral, on one side of Brīvības Iela stood an old wooden house. Neiburga's story harks back to the time of its former inhabitants; a time when there were more than 30 cinemas across the city, including Splendid Palace which stands on this same street today. Its classical architectural masterpieces also appear in Arno Jundze's story 'Killing Mrs Cecilia Bochs', exploring another phenomenon from the 1990s – the reclamation of newly privatised, former Soviet property after Latvia regained independence, and the controversial stories behind it.

Aleksandrs Čaks is a street running parallel to Brīvības Street and has its own distinctive atmosphere and stories of revelry. Kristīne Želve, in her story 'The Girl Who Cut My Hair', tells us of a neighbour who thinks he is a legend because he tells everyone that, as a boy, he had seen the poet Aleksandrs Čaks (a canonical poet from the 1930s). Maybe it was just his romantic imagination, prompted or inspired by the street's namesake.

This nostalgic atmosphere also pervades Gundega Repše's story 'Westside Garden' which takes us out of the city centre, through the Ziedonis, Latgale and Vērmane Gardens, the Brothers and Rainis Cemeteries – beautiful, green spaces on the right bank of the Daugava – the settings for rose gardens, and summer theatres with outdoor seating. The story takes place in Mežaparks (Kaiserwald Forest) which is often called the 'lungs of Riga'.

One of the most important buildings in Riga is situated on the left bank, the new Latvian National Library – known locally as 'The Castle of Light' or 'The Glass Mountain'. It is among the greatest cultural projects of the twenty-first century in Latvia. The symbolism and design of the building reference two iconic Latvian cultural metaphors. The first invokes a legend in which a great Castle of Light sank when the Latvian people were oppressed by several great powers, but then, from the depths of darkness, rose up again to free the Latvian nation. The second reference lies in the building's silhouette, being reminiscent of the legendary Glass Mountain, at the top of which a princess waits for her saviour – or at least someone brave enough to climb that high. Ilze Jansone, in her story 'Wonderful New Latvia', ironically reveals some alternative stories about the library and its design.

'The Birds of Ķīpsala Island' by Dace Rukšāne explores an island on the left bank of the Daugava. Ķīpsala is known for being a quiet place, resplendent with flora and fauna, modern and historical houses and narrow, romantic streets. The people and birds that live there all see themselves as islanders though they are only half a kilometre from Old Riga.

Vilis Lācītis uses the character of a writer, Spalvums, to explore another part of the left bank, called Āgenskalns, which is renowned for being the preserved wooden heart of Riga and a popular and eco-friendly place for creative people to live.

In 'The Night Shift', Pauls Bankovskis takes us to a darker part of Riga's history, retelling an urban legend about a blue bus in Riga that kidnaps children and takes them away to the forest, never to be seen again. The story is most likely based on the massacre of Riga's jews in Rumbula Forest in 1941: Jewish citizens were taken to the forest in bluish-grey transit buses. But in Bankovskis' story this was a route 3 bus from Bolderāja, a neighbourhood of Riga where the majority of the non-Latvian speaking population live, and this time the victims are the ticket conductors.

In 1837, shortly before leaving Berlin for Riga, the famous German composer Richard Wagner wrote to his wife: 'Riga is described to me as the nicest place in the world, especially when it comes to earning money...' The years that followed proved quite fruitful for him, from a creative point of view, though ultimately he had to leave due to unpaid bills and debts. Despite this, Riga is sometimes is called 'Wagner's city', and it has its stories about Wagner, just as Wagner did about Riga. The same could be said for everyone who lives and visits the city, and what follows is merely a selection of these. And as Kuzmin's 'The Shakes' notes, there is a special attachment between every writer and this city:

'Riga is just Riga, nothing out of the ordinary.'
'Maybe you just didn't notice, didn't pay any attention. It can be that way, too.'

'It can be that way, too' is the key phrase; there are many sides to Riga which its citizens walk past every day, sides that may or may not be being photographed by the tourists. Almost every single corner of Riga has its own story and *The Book of Riga* offers some of them up, and will hopefully lead you to many more.

Eva Eglāja-Kristsone,
Riga, February 2018

The Hare's Declaration

Juris Zvirgzdiņš

Translated by Mārta Ziemelis

IN SHORT, I LOST my job and didn't find a new one.

Wherever I tried to worm my way in: 'Sorry, you're just too old.' The bank took away my house, my wife left me, my daughters, well, go re-read *King Lear*, or *The Cat's Mill* by our very own Kārlis Skalbe – that's how they acted.

So then I decided to end it... loudly! I'd slam the door on the void with a bang! But before my exit, I'd say everything that was on my mind, and proudly. I didn't need the media, a TV debate or some internet forum getting in my way. They can't silence *me*!

I wandered aimlessly through Riga, looking for a place; the right place. The Freedom Monument? One guy already shot himself there. Does anyone still remember his name? The Vanšu Bridge? No, perhaps not. They'd trick me into coming down; they have enough money in their budget for that, you see. They'd send a smart-arse psychologist or the firemen... What about the tower of St. Peter's Church? The correct choice, sir, congratulations! That evening, with a backpack on my shoulders and my ticket in hand, I rode the lift to the tower's viewing platform. I listened a moment while a guide explained something to a group of Japanese tourists, then I crept off behind them up the metal stairs to the platform above. To be closer to the golden rooster weathervane and to God.

1

I spent the night in a sleeping bag. In the morning, I stood at the edge of the platform and – in order to attract attention – started waving my arms in the air. At first, only one passer-by raised their head, then another and another. Soon enough, a fairly large crowd of people had gathered below. A police car pulled up, then a fire engine and a crane. Striped tape was stretched out around the base of the tower.

I took the notepad containing my speech out of my backpack and raised my hand in greeting. I opened my mouth and... *sssh!* I could only whisper. My throat had closed up. I must have caught a cold, sleeping on the stone floor.

I tore the page out of my notepad, folded it into a paper airplane, and released it into the air. Spiralling, my declaration glided downward. A tall police officer jumped up and caught it. His commanding officer yanked the paper out of his hand, looked at it and, folding it carefully, stuffed it in the pocket of his uniform. He gave his subordinates an order. They formed a chain and shifted the crowd farther away from the church. Neither public outrage, nor eagerly flashed press ID's, were any good; the police let no one near. So, there I stood, waving my arms like a ghost, tearing pages from my notepad, scribbling this and that, then folding them into paper airplanes before throwing them into the crowds below. A few ended up in the cops' clutches, spectators collected others, and that was it. Nothing happened. No revolution began.

One after another, officials and psychologists tried to talk me down. A unit of men in bullet-proof vests tried to storm the tower, but my handmade poster near the platform – *LANDMINES!* – stopped them, and then they eventually got bored of trying. Even the helicopter didn't help; its blades got tangled in electrical wires and it crash-landed next to the Laima Clock, flattening the Lamborghini parked there. There were no casualties, thank God, and the car, unfortunately, was insured.

My humble food supply ran out within a few days. With a

packet of Selga cookies and the remnants of my mineral water, I figured I could last one more day. Two, at best.

What would I do next? Jump to the ground and shatter into a million pieces? Sneak down in the dark of night? Let them take me to the nuthouse and feed me pills? A splatter or a vegetable. I didn't have a lot of choices. What was holding me back? Arrogance? The desire not to disappoint my fans down there?

The crowd, always changing, grew in numbers. There were even bets being made: will he or won't he jump? Whole buses full of people appeared. I'd become a sensation, a tourist attraction and – to brag a bit – for much longer than Andy Warhol's promised fifteen minutes.

I wasn't bored. At night I could watch the city lights and gaze at the stars, and there was plenty to look at during the days too: here, a cluster of monks held a service, hands joined; there stood a lady I almost recognised, wearing a long coat with a huge hat, and surrounded by a police escort. She chanted into a megaphone: 'We are white as snow! We are colossal!' A crowd roared '*Bedovo*![1] Super!' in delight.

What saved me from hunger and thirst? School, the classics, Latvian literature. A quote went round and round my head: 'Don't request, demand!' It was maybe by Jānis Rainis, or perhaps even Vilis Plūdonis. 'Slam your fist on the table!' It's a shame there was no table.

I wrote my list of demands on the three pages left in my notepad, wrapped my shoelaces around it and lowered it to the floor below, where the guys in bullet-proof vests were on duty, a safe distance from my poster: *LANDMINES!* What did I demand? Some Hall's cough drops; a portable biological toilet and toilet paper (two-ply, extra-soft); breakfast, lunch and dinner made by celebrity chefs Mārtiņš Rītiņš and Mārtiņš Sirmais; and that the guards be removed from the viewing platform. I also demanded a megaphone; ten minutes of CNN

3

broadcasts per day (with a sign language interpreter and a ticker displaying English translations); meetings with the Dalai Lama, the Pope and Bill Gates; and, most importantly, two, no, maybe three éclairs with chocolate filling.

The Pope – God's representative on Earth – replied immediately, but evasively: he'd pray for me, and would send a cardinal in his place. I refused point-blank. It wasn't fitting for me – who stood so high up, almost at the very top of the tower – to speak to a representative's representative! The Dalai Lama was already on his way; he just had to go through his next incarnation. (Here, I think, our interpreters messed something up). Bill Gates sent me a computer so new even the Pentagon didn't have it yet, and a text message saying: SHIT HAPPENS! Maybe he'd been reading Vonnegut.

The guards left, and then the helicopters borrowed from Estonia lifted the portable biological toilet. The rest (toilet paper, Hall's cough drops, megaphone, and éclairs), I pulled up myself. The CNN broadcasters would come soon. Rītiņš and Sirmais really did know how to cook – over the next few days I ate like a guest at a wedding, and even gained weight! Everything was going swimmingly. I felt like those fat cats from Parex Bank, or at least like a member of the Saeima.

The rich food and sedentary life took its toll. My daily declaration – right at lunchtime – became tepid. Ratings fell. I started repeating myself; my jokes weren't funny anymore. I sensed the show approaching its end.

One night an unfamiliar noise startled me awake. Eyes wide, I saw the head of an uninvited guest appear just above the platform's edge. Tightly clutching the closest object (the megaphone), I quickly wriggled out of my sleeping bag. A figure, dressed in a blue and red outfit, and a hat embroidered with beads, approached.

'Well?' I waved my makeshift club threateningly. 'Talk... what do you want?'

'You... you speak Latvian? Mama told me only Russians live in Riga now!'

A woman, judging by the voice.

The stranger dropped her backpack, pulled out a piece of meat and handed it to me.

'Do you have a knife?'

'Yes!' I said.

The meat was tough, but edible.

'It's *poro!*'

'*Poro?*' I didn't understand.

'Polar deer!'

I understood and corrected: 'Reindeer? Where on earth did you come from?'

'I climbed up! We trolls climb very well, you see.'

'Trolls?'

'Well... Papa's a troll, but Mama's a Latvian from Ventspils.'

'A troll?' I repeated. I'd seen trolls in my childhood, in pictures in my mother's book *Peer Gynt*.

'Look! Like all trolls I have four fingers!' Tugging with her teeth, she took off a leather glove and held out her palm toward me, looking closely to see if I believed her or not.

'A joke!' She laughed. 'My father's no troll; my finger was torn off when I was little, riding in a sleigh. My father's a Sami. Have you read Knut Hamsun?'

'Umm...'

'There's a Sami in his work called Gilbert. That was my very rich grandfather. Our family owns *tuhat poroa*, a thousand deer! No, *kymmenentuhatta poroa*. Ten thousand polar deer! Believe me, we'll be a wealthy couple.'

'We?' Again, I didn't understand.

'Well... *nyt kyllä nain sinut!*' she said. 'I'm going to marry you!'

'But why?' I no longer understood anything. Was this woman really offering to marry me?

5

'Because you're the right one for me, OK? I saw you on TV!' She paused: 'Any objections?'

Something cawed behind me. I turned my head. Two massive black birds were hovering in the air, ravens.

'Shoo! Shoo!' My guest drove them away. 'They're *Huginn* – Thought – and *Muninn* – Memory. Odin's ravens! My name's Sunna, what's yours?'

'Jānis!' I replied. What other name can a Latvian have?

Sunna laughed. 'Jānis! Really! In Finnish that means "hare"!'[2]

Done laughing, she pulled a small birchbark box from her bag, opened it carefully, poured a pinch of powder into her palm, snorted it and handed me the box.

'*Kärpässienet!*'

I didn't understand.

'Mushrooms. Those red ones with white spots!'

'Toadstools?'

'Yes!'

I snorted some. Might as well.

'Well?'

What else was left to do? I shrugged, then nodded my head.

Our conversation continued on a horizontal level. She radiated heat.

Suddenly the ravens cawed louder. Was I seeing things? Yes, I was. A sleigh pulled by reindeer approached, with helicopter propellers attached and SAMPO[3] written on the side. It stopped at the edge of the platform. A man wearing a little red cap – maybe a troll – sat at the controls. He wore leather gloves, I couldn't see how many fingers he had...

'Let's go!' Sunna urged.

She pushed me into the sleigh, then climbed in herself. The giant dragonfly roared and rose into the air.

'Where are we flying to?' I asked, though, honestly, I didn't care.

'What do you mean, where? To Lapland, of course!'

I nodded. Yes, to Lapland, naturally.

'Only...' here Sunna's white teeth dazzled me, 'on the way, we'll drop in at a place where you'll be able to read out your HARE'S DECLARATION!'

Notes

1. Russian for 'Great!'

2. In Latvian fairytales, the hare (or rabbit) is a signifier or representation of cowardice.

3. In Finnish myth (specifically the epic poem 'The Kalevala'), the Sampo was a magical artifact of indeterminate type, made by the smith Ilmarinen, that brought wealth and good fortune to its holder.

The Birds of Ķīpsala Island

Dace Rukšāne

Translated by Žanete Vēvere Pasqualini

HOOPOE

IF TRUTH BE TOLD, this is a strange place to live. These recently erected, semi-detached houses on Enkuru Street. Straight hedges, straight houses, too; each one the same as the next with tiny courtyards squeezed tightly together, like lockers in a gym changing room. My garden is visible to the neighbours and, in turn, I can see the perfect lawn to the left, and the dog-holed garden of my neighbour to the right. On one side, I have the Bernese mountain dog, on the other, a poor Siberian husky who has nothing better to do than dig up the lawn and make regular bids for escape. If anyone has a barbecue on a Friday evening you can hear the babble of conversation three doors down, so generally the neighbours all organise barbeques at the same time. That way, everybody just listens to their own conversations, and no one worries about being overheard.

Nevertheless, as my husband points out to me, living like this is perfectly normal. Indeed, most families in the West live in this exact same way. 'Middle management,' he says, in his broken Latvian. 'With children,' he adds and disappears once more into his computer, banging on the keyboard with such force I fear it will break.

I know everybody else around has children, damn it! It's the very reason why he rented this house for us. To give us space for children. Right next to the school. Foreign children really should attend a school for foreigners. It's essential.

Agreed, but we are not middle management. My husband earns much more than most, whereas I am an artist. And I don't want children for now. I don't want *any* children.

I am suffocating enough as it is; in these squares, these concrete paving slabs with neat greenery, and the unchanging view from my window where all you can see is the window of the house opposite, and another lawn that looks no different from the lawns on either side.

All the neighbours round here are really friendly. Every day they smile at me, dishing out trite greetings as we cross paths, organising parties together where they pull their barbeques out onto the street and join forces to burn sausages. Nobody drinks anything stronger than orange juice. No one ever dares to get into an argument, drag themselves home legless, snip neighbours' rhododendrons, kiss in their car out front, sing loudly, or even fail to pull up the country's flag on national holidays. These are family homes, and the families in them are exemplary, or so they think.

If we don't come to blows over a conversation about kids, my husband broaches the subject of my painting.

'Why aren't you doing anything? Why haven't you painted anything yet? I bought you a new easel, all brand new brushes, gallons of paint, and that room is all for you – yours, yours, yours – no one else goes in it! So why aren't you painting? I haven't seen a single work! Do you even know what you really want?'

At times like these, I get sad and walk straight out the door. Turn right, turn right, right again, go on a bit, then slightly left until I reach the old chalk factory complex. It has been stylishly renovated and turned into expensive, multi-storey apartments;

the enormous chimney still standing right at its heart. Now home to the renowned and sophisticated Fabrikas restaurant, it's the place where the islands' well-to-do residents, and various arty types, gather at weekends. It is the only spot on the whole island where you can have a drink in peace without needing to hide from the neighbours. If I suspect my husband might turn up looking for me, I ask the waiter to serve me some wine into a teacup and pass me a few sprigs of mint. The staff have long since got used to my jokes about this and we don't even laugh at them anymore. When my husband appears in the doorway, the waiter says, 'Madam is expecting you,' and helps him out of his coat while telling him what's new on the wine list, as well as the chef's special. The barman begins to talk about the lovely or appalling weather we are having and the upcoming parliamentary session. Thus, they work to delay my husband. Just to give me a few moments to chew on the mint sprigs.

When he is on a business trip, I drink wine openly. I soak it up like a leech, and don't unlatch myself until I'm full to the gills with it. By that time, it's usually dark enough for me to crawl home as I please – the neighbours wouldn't be up that late to see me anyhow, they'd all be fast asleep.

I swear that I'd start painting again if, for just a week, he would stop going on about either children or the easel. I would start painting those little bricks, those small squares even, moving seamlessly on to those wonderful, exceptional skies, which you can't find anywhere else but here. I would paint kaleidoscopic watercolours, with half shades and the nuances of local folk. I swear I would, but my vow echoes like an empty tin can, as my husband can never go longer than a week without nagging.

And I swear, I swear that I would have children if only my husband... if only my husband wasn't my husband.

'Why do you live with him?' the barman asks.

'To have the time, the space and the chance to paint.'

11

'And do you have the time?'
'Yes.'
'Do you have the space?'
'A whole large room.'
'And do you have the chance?'
'Whenever I want.'
'Then why don't you paint?'
'Because I live with him.'

This is a kind of game for us. The same questions over and over, the same answers.

On one occasion, I decide to change the rules of the game. The usual question, 'Then why don't you paint', is followed by the answer: 'Because I never get home to find a hoopoe with the colours of a Dzungarian tiger sitting on the gate post.'

The barman is awestruck, I'm sozzled. We shag in the overgrown apple orchard of a derelict house, and the following day I paint my first painting in five years. Of course, my husband is beside himself.

Two weeks later, I'm in a panic, the barman is flabbergasted again, and my husband is blissfully unaware that my period is late.

I'm painting like mad, but I can't work out how to get out of this one. I later read online that it is hamsters rather than tigers that come from Dzungaria. The tigers come from Wusuli. The hoopoe is an extremely attractive bird with a folding crest, nevertheless.

THE CUCKOO'S NEST

I had fallen in love with Ķīpsala Island back when I was really small. I used to ride across the newly built suspension bridge and go off on lone forays into the island's scrublands, through the shabby houses with rickety fencing round their gardens filled with stray animals. I would set off along its coastline,

12

finding puddles from which I would fish out dragonfly larvae to store in jars, so I could watch them hatch. I wandered along cobbled streets and through mudbanks, along sandy paths and tarmacked squares, tripping across grassy meadows and dog-fouled tracks. I chatted to harmless old winos and shared cigarettes with exhausted, fierce young women, but would always beat a hasty retreat as soon as I caught sight of any drunken youngsters in the distance.

I used to take my first boyfriends there to kiss, talk and knock back a drink or two from my hip flask. When I started to have boyfriends with cars, we would go to the remote roads and lanes of Ķīpsala, again because, unlike Zaķusala Island and the hippodrome jungle, the police never made an appearance there. Later, officers in patrol cars used to ask for a tenner in return for not reporting acts of public indecency.

The cover of a famous Latvian novel featured a picture of a graffiti-smothered brick wall in Ķīpsala, bearing slogans like 'ĶĪPSALA IS A LAND OF WINOS. JUST LIE BACK AND SOAK UP THE BOOZE.' Below, another hand had scrawled, 'IT'S AN ISLAND OF LOVE, TOO.' And you could just make out 'ĶĪPSALA IS A FORCE!' daubed in Russian alongside it. Everything the graffiti said was true. I searched all over the island for the house featured in the story, but never found it. There are no such shrubs on that island in bloom, no such house to be found.

This made me feel both disappointed and delighted in equal measure. It meant that writers gabbled nonsense just like everyone else, and that most tear-jerkers were therefore probably no more than the fruit of someone's fervid imagination. In reality, life is not that harsh, it really isn't. Of course, it also follows that no one in real life is as happy, as witty, or as capable of making sound judgements, as characters in fiction.

It might be said that a writer could turn my own situation into some kind of soppy drama featuring a woman who has suffered endlessly with rotten men at her side. On the other hand, I could also be portrayed as a mean old cow. In fact, everything was quite simple the first time round. And the second. My first husband picked me up, all tender and innocent, threw me into his lair and kept me there. I only ever saw him late at night and sometimes not at all. When I got pregnant, he threw me out, because, as it transpired, he was actually infertile. To avoid comparisons with movie plots, I will add that it was neither the pool cleaner, the plumber or the floor waxer. Just an old classmate of mine who didn't find it so very difficult to talk to me. Over the three previous years, he had been the only one to go beyond small talk. I couldn't invite any of my girlfriends back to the lair. Not unless I wanted them to be so envious they would end up wishing me ill.

My second child was stolen, too, if I can put it that way. I fell madly in love. I chose the most common and maybe only available option, just as lonely women with a child often do – a happily married man. The sort with whom there isn't the smallest glimmer of hope. He was so handsome, so clever, so kind, so healthy, so faithful to his wife that I resolved that a genetic combination such as ours shouldn't be passed up. You have to grab at miracles like these when they come along; there's so much rubbish floating about, so much genetic material gone wrong. My son came out perfectly calculated, planned and completely anonymous. His father still has no idea of his existence. I have only told one girlfriend about him (in case something happens to me). So long as she never lets the cat out of the bag in a sudden surge of emotion, his father will never know. I'll tell my son when he is sixteen. Or maybe eighteen. Then he can decide for himself.

I had received a good education before my children were born and found a good job when I was expecting my first child. My first husband turned out to be quite a decent type and didn't leave me totally without means. He told me I deserved it 'for the years I had devoted to our marriage' and 'because he had been at home so rarely.' I almost regret that my first child doesn't have his genes – such nobleness is quite uncommon these days; I should have immortalised it.

My girlfriends dream of living in all kinds of other places – Mežaparks, Jūrmala, Tenerife, even London – whereas I've been dreaming of living on Ķīpsala Island for as long as I can remember, even though there wasn't really anywhere to live on it back then; the whole place was falling apart. Nowadays, you have quite a lot of choice. Some people are moving in, some are leaving to find somewhere better, some can't make their mortgage repayments. Two weeks ago, I was on my usual rounds of Ķīpsala with my little ones, studying the notices on the houses: *For Sale, For Rent, For Sale, For Rent.*

I've managed to realise most of my dreams – a daughter, a son, a job, money, friends too. I even go windsurfing sometimes. It seems that now is the right time to fulfil my wish of living on Ķīpsala Island. The main thing is to get moved into a place and get on with living there – better still if it is cheap. Then I will look around, take stock and decide where to settle down for good. The cheapest solution would no doubt be the row of semi-detached houses. That sort of home would be quite acceptable – a small yard, a quiet street for the little ones to play out in, enough space in the garage for the car and a surfboard.

After checking out the houses on offer from the outside, I choose the one which seems to have the most decent yard. I call on the neighbours and ask what it's like living there. In one house they are incredibly kind, inviting me in and showing me the layout, pointing out that it's much the same as the house on offer. Although, the tenants there were apparently quite out of their minds, especially the woman ('probably an artist'). At times she got dressed up like a bird, at others like a scarecrow. She used to run around the island like a headless chicken, singing loudly at night and not making friends with any of the neighbours. It was said she spent more time at the bar than at the stove. The barman must have had something to do with it. Nothing stays a secret here on the island. The husband, quite a run-of-the-mill sort of man, had probably just had enough and threw her out of the house. And not quietly, but with the sort of shouting and yelling that they simply weren't used to round here. All quite unacceptable. He had grabbed hold of her from behind, dragged her right across the yard and shoved her out of the gate. Then, he had thrown all her clothes, bags, brushes, an easel, suitcases, flowerpots and even some chairs over the fence. Mad as a hatter. Shouting the whole time; some of it in English, some of it in French and the occasional German, too. The poor creature would have spent the whole night sitting by the fence if it hadn't been for us, her closest neighbours, taking her in. We made her some tea, dropped some valerian extract in her mouth, leant her our phone to call her sister. Her old man had smashed hers to pieces on the concrete pavement. We had heard something about her expecting a child. Not her husband's, more likely than not, if that's how it ended up. All this happened two weeks ago. Look, you can still see bits of broken clay all over the place; must be from those flowerpots. She was very good with anthuriums.

Not long later, I key in the number from the sign on the wall of the house. The landlord and I set up a meeting.

'Why so cheap?' I ask, already at the gate.

'I haven't had time to give it a going over. It's exactly as the previous tenants left it. I'm just not up to it.'

'Is it really that bad? You don't usually get complete and utter pigs as tenants in this part of town.'

'Why don't you go see for yourself. I am lucky to have found you! The old tenants just ran away as fast as they could, without so much as a by-your-leave, but look, I already have a new tenant to replace them! I'd already resigned myself to losing six-months' rent. You know, these days me and my wife's pensions... Tell you what, if you do it up yourself, I could let you live here rent-free for the first two months...'

I go in. Entrance hall, kitchen, living room. All quite normal, clean, even fresh feeling. I give the owner an inquisitive look.

'Go upstairs,' he says, sitting down on the bottom stair.

I go up to the first floor. There it is. The artist's room. Her nest. It's thronging with birds, floor to ceiling. Birds on the walls, birds on the floor, the entire ceiling is covered with birds. There are native grey ones as well as bright, exotic ones: swans and martins, wrens and orioles, quails, ruffs, hoopoes and baldicoots, not to mention goldfinches, Eurasian tree creepers, hedge sparrows and finches. Gathered together from all over, pampered and assembled in one little den. Every one of them cherished and nursed, each one in its own place. It will take a week or more to survey and name them. It will take half a lifetime to get to know them all.

'I'm taking the house,' I tell the landlord. 'It's almost as if it's been waiting for my children and me all this time.'

The Shakes

Sven Kuzmins

Translated by Žanete Vēvere Pasqualini

FROM VERY EARLY MORNING, Agnia found herself victim to a hard-to-explain, almost irrational anxiety. Everything had seemed to be going so wonderfully. No complications at work; Mr Jensen was happy with everything; no health issues; her body weight was ideal; the new apartment light and spacious, her financial situation more than satisfying. And yet somewhere, underneath it all, a tiny cell was hiding – Agnia referred to it as a cell – which wouldn't let her relax. *Perhaps it's all down to the changeable weather*, she reflected, searching for an explanation while sitting at the breakfast table, unable to concentrate on the book which lay next to her. Her glance kept returning to the start of the passage: 'Having been accepted into the elite, Knecht's life was elevated to another level, he had made the first – the most decisive – step in his growth.' Realising that she would make no such progress, Agnia closed the book and put it in her bag, poured the dregs of her coffee down the sink and left for work.

But even there she could find no peace; it seemed that something unexpected was about to happen any minute. *Maybe my life is just too comfortable*, she thought to herself, and got on with tackling Mr Jensen's incoming mail.

Soon the somewhat redundant telephone on her desk rang. Redundant as it was connected directly to Mr Jensen's office, situated just the other side of the wall. Fingers tapping nervously on the desktop, Agnia picked up the receiver.

'Good morning, Agnia,' Jensen said. 'Please come in to my office a moment.' His voice could be heard coming straight through the wall. A second later, it echoed down the receiver. Something was not right; the boss never called her in needlessly, even his coffee was always ordered over the phone. She got up and slowly opened the door to Mr Jensen's office, just one step away.

'Good morning,' she said, trying to sound as normal as possible.

'Hi. You look great today,' Jensen remarked. His disarming smile and barely noticeable Swedish accent somehow made his words more convincing, only adding to Agnia's nerves.

'Thank you!' she mumbled, deep down awaiting the bad news, whatever it was, which was sure to follow. But Jensen just ran his fingers through his white hair and gestured for her to sit.

'This won't take long,' he said and Agnia felt her skin prickle with goose bumps.

Jensen paused, as if trying to find the best way to put what he had to say.

'What's your favourite wine?' he asked.

'Wine?'

'Yes, what kind of wine? Red?'

'Yes, red.'

'So red it is. Jolly good. What kind of red? Dry?'

'Dry is nice.' Agnia wasn't sure if that was the right answer. Besides, she didn't actually like wine. She much preferred prosecco.

'Lovely. I want you to run down to *Vīna Studija* and get us a couple of bottles of dry red wine.'

'I really don't know very much about wine,' she confessed.

'Then go by the label: the prettier the label, the better the wine.'

'Fine. What time for?'

Jensen laughed.

'It's quite horrifying how I've got you to toe the line! Quite horrible!' he said. 'Half past four. Let's say that today we're knocking off early. We've worked hard and now we can afford to treat ourselves to a nicely labelled bottle of wine.'

'Right. Dry red wine for half past four.' Agnia jotted in her diary, surprised that Jensen would want to have a drink with her. Up until then, nothing like that had ever happened.

'You don't look in the least bit pleased,' Mr Jensen concluded, which served to add to her state of confusion. She racked her brains for a suitable answer, but Jensen cut in, 'Don't worry, there won't be any awkward little chats with the boss, if that's what's worrying you.'

'No, nothing of the kind,' Agnia tried to justify herself.

'It's alright. As you say. The main thing is – be here at half past four with wine.'

'Agreed,' Agnia smiled without feeling much relieved. Something still wasn't right. Jensen was certainly very punctual by nature but really – why exactly at half past four? With Jensen's permission, she went back to work.

'Ah, and another thing,' he suddenly exclaimed as Agnia opened the door. She took a step back and looked inquiringly at her boss. So, here was the bad news.

'Make me a banana milkshake, please.'

'Sure, coming up,' Agnia nodded.

'Thank you,' Jensen smiled. 'I didn't have time for breakfast today and my brain is like a motor. It needs loads of calories to run.'

'So they say,' she nodded once more and took one short step back into her small adjoining room.

Just before half past four, while Agnia was expecting Jensen's call and killing time by trying to read her book, the boss took her by surprise by popping his head round the office door.

'Hi, you're just waiting for me to call, aren't you? Come on in.'

Agnia put down her book on the desk.

'How interesting!' he said. 'I didn't know you were a literature buff. Can I ask what you are reading?'

'*The Glass Bead Game.*'

'Ah, Hesse. And do you like it?'

'To be honest, I'm finding it very slow,' Agnia admitted. 'I much preferred *Steppenwolf.*'

'Yes, I totally agree,' her boss said. 'I couldn't get past the foreword. You know, I felt sorry for modern civilisation. He predicted such a gloomy decline for us, didn't he?'

'I don't know. I thought he was rather trying to describe the superficial nature of modern civilisation but then just sank into generic, primitive romanticism,' Agnia confessed, unable to believe that she was speaking with her boss about the decline of civilisation instead of meetings and money.

'Hmm. Maybe it was his supercilious tone to kill any enjoyment I had in reading him. Alright, show me what you bought,' Jensen said and opened his office door in invitation. Agnia picked up the wine merchant's shopper and followed him inside.

'Nice choice,' he said filling their glasses. 'Really nice.'

'I went by the labels and prices.'

'Ha-ha. That always works well. Cheers!' he toasted, chinking glasses with his assistant.

For a while, they stayed sitting in the leather armchairs, sipping wine and saying nothing and yet, contrary to expectations, the silence wasn't awkward. Agnia was scanning Jensen's office from an unusual perspective which revealed details she hadn't previously had time to notice: the paintings on the wood-panelled walls, pen and ink drawings, book shelves, decorative plates, sculptures and sports trophies. Jensen looked at his watch.

'Ah, it's about to begin,' he said, refilling his wine glass and going over to the window.

'What is?'

'Come and see,' Jensen drew back the heavy velvet curtains. At first, Agnia couldn't see anything out of the ordinary – *Vec Riga* – Old Riga just as it always was – cobbled pavement, shops, restaurants, a little further off the Castle Square. There were still months to go until the tourist season started, so it was all quite peaceful, almost pleasant-looking. But then, a small group of people appeared on the street, heading towards Castle Square and Jensen, glancing at his watch again, said, 'Yes, it's started.'

The small assembly had stopped on the edge of the pavement and was unpacking their gear onto the lawn – pieces of fabric and rolled-up placards which had been shoved into their bags. Painted in bright acrylic colours, carrying placards of varying levels of wit and printing quality, these were distributed among the group who then slowly started pacing the square. Agnia had already summed up this improvised demonstration as rather pitiful, but Jensen meanwhile observed the course of events eagerly, as if he had put stakes on one of the participants in the demonstration. Another ten or fifteen minutes went by and the scant group gradually grew into a smallish crowd, being joined all the time by a steady stream of people. They yelled something and, growing increasingly animated, waved their placards in the direction of the castle.

'Look, watch how precisely it all works out,' Jensen said, sounding satisfied. 'It's like a well-oiled machine.'

'How do you mean?' Agnia couldn't see what he was so happy about. 'Was it pre-arranged somehow?'

'What exactly?' Jensen asked again, the falling intonation so characteristic of his speech was strong.

'The demonstration.'

'There must have been some sort of organisation behind it, but I didn't follow that especially.'

'But you must have known something about it? Surely!'

Jensen took another sip without taking his eyes off the window.

'I didn't have to know anything,' he said. 'It's all one hundred per cent predictable. Or did you think that your conservative government's doings would go no further than television talk shows and the online news? That the respectable populace would continue not to speak up? Forget it.' Jensen gave Agnia a smile and she put her glass to her lips as if to apologise.

'I know what you're thinking,' he said. 'How on earth could he have known. You are, aren't you? Isn't it some sort of conspiracy?'

'I am not thinking of conspiracies,' Agnia said. 'And I wouldn't do, either, unless you gave me some reason to think otherwise. But such a precise forecast of events...'

Jensen laughed.

'It's not as complicated as it might seem. It doesn't take a political scientist to realise all is not quite right, does it? It is in the general mood, it can be felt.'

He looked at Agnia as if waiting for her confirmation.

'My grandfather worked on the fishing ships,' Jensen continued. 'Near Öland. And he was always, always able to tell when the herring would spawn. As a boy, when I asked him how he knew, he answered, "The water is restless today," and carried on smoking his pipe. I kept on staring at the water's surface but didn't sense a thing – the sea was just the sea, nothing out of the ordinary.'

'I didn't sense a thing. Riga was just Riga, nothing out of the ordinary.'

'Maybe you just didn't notice, didn't pay any attention. It can be that way, too,' Jensen said, and continued watching the unfolding of events in the square.

Meanwhile, the group had grown into a considerable crowd which had spread to cover the whole square, from the church of Our Lady of Sorrows, *Sāpju Dievmātes*, as far as the Castle Tower. Pairs of police officers patrolled the square uneasily, murmuring into their radios.

'Interesting,' Agnia commented. 'Usually in Latvia, no one has much inclination to think about such things. It's just our national mindset, I suppose.'

'No, no, no,' Jensen cut her short. 'It has nothing to do with mindset. I know what you mean. The last serious demonstration in Riga was back in 2008 and even then, the most serious incident was somebody throwing a couple of cobblestones in the direction of the Saeima.[1] It was nothing, was it?'

'More or less.'

'Exactly,' Jensen concluded, jabbing his finger triumphantly on the windowpane. 'And I can bet that your honourable politicians think exactly the same way. That this isn't Paris, nobody here is going to burn any tyres or upturn any cars. And all of that is based on the assumption —'

'That Latvians are not like that?'

'Yes. Yes, yes, yes. I couldn't put it better myself. That Latvians are simply not "like that". But with just a little thought you'll come to realise that such an assumption is based not on real experience but rather on the absence of such experience. And it's a very, very dangerous trap to fall into.'

'And how to avoid falling into such a trap?' Agnia asked incredulously.

'An excellent question, Agnia. It's like iron; heat it to a certain temperature and it starts glowing different colours — first red, then white. But you can't simply feel the temperature with your hand. It's more or less the same thing here. I don't know, maybe these metaphors aren't working. Everything boils down to the fact that you just need to feel it.'

'Metaphors are fine but unfortunately feelings don't form a rational argument.'

'Yes, and political ethics is often neither rational nor convenient when seen from the standpoint of immediate practicality. And this is the result.'

'In that case, what is happening on the other side of this window – is it a white or red glow?'

'These are still barely warmed-up coals, Agnia,' Jensen smiled, sighing as he did so.

Agnia didn't know how to respond. She watched as police officers on motorcycles re-routed the traffic and wondered whether she might have preferred staying at home that day, reading *The Glass Bead Game*.

'You are not drinking your wine?' Jensen broke the moment of silence.

'Sorry, I was lost in thought.'

'You don't have to apologise. You don't like red wine, do you? Just in case, there is some prosecco in the sideboard. I'll pour you some.' He smiled politely and took the half-empty wine glass from Agnia's hand.

The conversation came to an end with Jensen apologising to Agnia for taking up her time and saying she was free to go home. Saturday came but, despite it being the first warm day of the year, Agnia cancelled her brunch date with friends and didn't go to yoga either; she had felt tired and empty all morning. Instead, she sat by the window and read the bulky novel she still hadn't really got into, every so often raising her eyes to look out the window at the wall of the derelict factory, warmed by the afternoon sun. *Do I feel anything out of the ordinary?* she mused. Apart from the unaccounted for anxiousness, all she felt was a certain languor and sluggishness... and that was nothing out of the ordinary.

On Monday morning, Jensen behaved as if their conversation had never taken place. He asked Agnia to make him a banana milkshake and, with his customary earnestness, got on with tackling the day-to-day paperwork, meetings and telephone calls – and Agnia helped him as enthusiastically as usual. At the end of the day though, when she was ready to go home, Jensen called his assistant into his office.

'Listen, I was thinking all weekend about how we should proceed, but I still need a little longer. Could you please get someone to install over there' – he pointed to the wall on the opposite side of the office – 'one of those white backdrop screens you get in photographic studios?'

'A backdrop screen?'

'Yes, you know, one of those large, roll-up paper things.'

'OK, fine. When do you need it for?' Agnia clarified.

'ASAP. We don't have much time,' Jensen replied, biting the end of his pen.

Agnia nodded and wrote a note in her diary.

By midweek, the far wall of Jensen's office had been cleared of paintings and shelves of trophies and a huge cylinder holding a roll of paper was screwed above directly into the ceiling. Jensen was delighted with this new purchase. He unfurled the paper sheet right down, covering most of the wall, and then fixed it to the skirting board with the latch provided.

'Wonderful,' he said when the men who had come to install it had left his office. 'Thank you, Agnia, you can go home, too.'

'Really?' Agnia asked uncertainly, 'It's not even two o'clock yet and tomorrow we have –'

'Yes, yes, I know. A conference with the Germans. Cancel it.'

He frowned and scrutinised Agnia, deep in thought.

'Listen, when did you last take a holiday?'

'I don't think this is a good time.'

'I won't hear of it. As of now, you have two weeks' paid

leave. Fill in the paperwork now and go home.'

'But what about the Germans? We've been waiting for them for so long to –'

'Again, I won't hear of it. You have to rest. Go, go,' Jensen added hastily, gesturing that she was to leave him alone that instant.

With each passing day, the city air became increasingly oppressive and yet the storm didn't break. Agnia stayed at home, soon coming to the conclusion that such a holiday was more like exile. *It wouldn't hurt if I went somewhere, even just to Sigulda or Cyprus maybe*, she thought, but the same disagreeable sense of unease continued to gnaw in her chest. With every passing day it became more and more overwhelming, almost bone-crushingly so. The feeling that she shouldn't go anywhere didn't leave her for a second; that she shouldn't move just in case Jensen needed anything, even though he hadn't answered any of her calls for the past week. Agnia had given this feeling of hers a name – the Shakes – thinking that if it went on much longer she would have to go for counselling. She was making slow progress with *The Glass Bead Game* and in fact it was increasingly getting on her nerves with each page she read. In the meantime, the wall of the derelict factory was getting warmer and warmer in the spring sunshine. At times, she imagined white-hot bricks coming into contact with a much longed-for shower of cool water, there would be a loud hiss and clouds of steam would rise into the air. After the rain the air would be fresh and healing. As she breathed it in, the Shakes would leave her mind and body where she stood. Over the past two weeks, practically nothing else had been worthy of her consideration.

At eight o'clock the next morning, Agnia knocked on Jensen's door.

'What are you doing here?' he exclaimed, having popped his head round the opening. 'Didn't I tell you to take leave?'

'Yes, you did and the two weeks are up.'

'Really? So soon. I hadn't noticed. Alright, come in.'

The heavy curtains were drawn, the ceiling light was on and an unpleasant, sour smell hung in the air. Besides which, Jensen obviously hadn't shaved in all that time and his cheeks were covered evenly with a white beard. Under any other circumstances, Agnia would have said that he looked much better like that, but he still had the same suit on which he had been wearing two weeks ago and there was something wrong with his eyes – they appeared to have sunk deep into their sockets and were a little inflamed. Most of all, Agnia's attention was captured by the backdrop screen. At first glance, it seemed to be covered in blue fabric. Yet following Jensen's invitation to move closer, she was totally aghast. Intricately and painstakingly, Jensen had covered the whole screen with a blue meshwork of thick lines, some sort of a rough knitting pattern, and only by bending down to view it up close could she see that each thread in this faultless meshwork was filled with incredibly fine text. She turned towards Jensen who was standing behind her and he smiled, as if expecting her approval. Agnia tried to find the right words but Jensen was wriggling his fingers so impatiently that all she managed to utter awkwardly was: 'What is it?'

'It's a Scheme.' Jensen explained in a strange, tired voice that sounded much deeper than usual.

'A Scheme for what?'

'Not for what, but *why*. To understand what exactly goes wrong in any exact place and at any exact time you have to consider thousands of factors, do you follow me? Those people that went out onto the streets didn't do so without good reason.'

'Of course, I think we already cleared that up.'

'Yes, they were not satisfied. And why were they dissatisfied? Because no man in his right state of mind would be happy with your government's work,' Jensen kept talking faster and faster and was tracing the word thread on the paper with his finger. 'But why is your government the way it is? Why have people started to react only now, and not, let's say, when the real estate bubble burst? Do you understand that you have to consider not tens, not hundreds, but millions of factors? Reality does not comprise history and culture alone. Reality is like a meshwork woven of countless threads, Agnia. I've made an approximate sketch of it here.'

'What did you sketch? Reality?'

'No, not reality. In spite of what you might think, I haven't gone mad. No. This is just a model of reality. You see, here I've drawn all the threads I could think of,' Jensen continued, with passion, 'Nature, family, science and God, ethics and war, art and music, sensibility and cynicism, it's all here, and it all comes together in a perfect weave which represents reality in one combined scheme.'

'Then where is the problem?' Agnia asked, interpreting Jensen's pause correctly as a big 'but'.

'Agnia, the problem is here,' he said and pulled down the paper roll. No less than another eight metres of equally perfect patterns covering the entire enormous expanse unfurled from the cylinder. Jensen pointed to a small dot in the upper right-hand corner of the sheet, 'Here, there is a hole in my meshwork. The threads won't come together. This can only mean that, in that time and place, there is going to be an even greater uprising.'

Jensen paused again before collapsing with a sigh into a leather armchair.

'There is going to be a greater uprising,' he continued, 'I felt it before, but now I know. This is already a red glow.'

'Well, let's assume...' Agnia wanted to interrupt him but Jensen wasn't listening.

'And it's no wonder. Maybe if your society was a little

more united it could be avoided somehow. The problem is that you are too proud. For twenty-five years you have been purposefully splitting society in two. Dividing, dividing, until it split, and common sense didn't correspond with the nineteenth-century ideal you had cherished in your imagination. The only surprising thing in all of this is that you yourselves didn't sense this moment approaching. You had time to put things right but now it's too late. Soon it's going to be worse here than Maidan in Ukraine.[2] There's no excluding the fact that we are the only two people who know, to be one hundred per cent convinced of what's going to happen next.'

'We? What do you mean by we?'

'You and me,' Jensen replied, as if it had been obvious from the start, 'and that means that if we don't take prompt action, the peaceful demonstration will be replaced by an armed coup. And believe you me, it's not going to be a pleasant sight to be watched with a glass of wine. It will be a bloody, horrifying performance by the theatre of magic. Just like every other civil war in world history, this is going to be no different.'

'How can we change it for the better?'

'I don't know, Agnia, but it's imperative that we come up with something. Traditional methods will be of no help here anymore,' Jensen said, thoughtful and sad, as he got up and went over to the window. He yanked back the curtains and opened the window but the air outside was even heavier than inside the office.

Jensen fell silent and Agnia slid unnoticed out of the office, realising it was time to get back to work. She really wanted to believe that Jensen had gone crazy and yet he appeared totally rational. *What if he's right?* Agnia thought. *What if everything really is as dreadful as he says?* She bit her lip. The Shakes gained strength. Now they were running in waves across her shoulders right down to her heels and back again. The only thing she wanted was for it to stop. She sat down and put her head in her hands. Up until then, her duties had been limited to office management. Nobody had taught her how to stop civil wars and avoid state coups. She sat stock still and felt herself slowly sinking into despair. At that moment, Jensen called on the phone.

'Listen, Agnia, don't you worry. We'll sort out the other stuff later. Could I ask you to make me one of your wonderful banana milkshakes?' Suddenly Jensen was back, talking in his normal voice, 'And set up that meeting with the Germans. I've got a feeling it's going to be the best deal of the year.'

Shortly afterwards he had showered, shaved, changed his clothes, rolled his reality meshwork back into its cylinder and tasked Agnia with a load of papers, e-mails and phone calls. He was back to being the same decisive, energetic Swedish entrepreneur whose sensible judgements Agnia trusted so much.

Notes

1. The Saeima is the parliament of the Republic of Latvia.
2. In 2014, demonstrators gathered in Kiev's main square for three months to protest against the government of President Viktor Yanukovych, who soon afterwards fled the country.

Westside Garden

Gundega Repše

Translated by Kaija Straumanis

I'M FINE. LEAVE ME ALONE! I'm sleeping. Stop knocking on my door. I'm not going to open it. You're wasting your time. Call the police, the landlord, the neighbourhood watch, Special Forces, the Black Berets – I won't open it. Kick it in, knock it down, go ahead! I'm sleeping, slee-ping. And that's that. You want to tie me up, throw me out? But where? By the gate? Inside or outside? My name's not Verona, you hear me, Ļusja? It's Veronika. And stop yelling, Vlad. I'm not scared of you. I'm not scared of anything. And leave Old Oto alone, he's not a bad guy! Tell Mrs Ozers to write to the newspaper, it'll be more accurate that way. And in French, of course. She probably only knows how to write in Russian using Early Cyrillic – she's ancient! I'm slee-ping! Stop it! And don't peek through the keyhole, Ļusja. I recognise those flared nostrils, thinking about your little Ira. Leave me alone! I'm fine, and I'm not going to open the door. I live here. Live *here*. Do you understand?

*

That's my mother, all dressed up in the long, pale-yellow gown with the fancy belt embroidered in white; she's looking over the table that has been set out on the stone terrace. Her face is flushed. Her dark-blonde hair is pinned up in a neat, soft bun

33

that I want to bury my face in so that it tickles my nose. She is calm and gentle, often daydreaming. Father is so absorbed in his newspapers it's almost as if we're not expecting guests. He's wearing his Sunday suit – he looks serious, stern and, it seems to me, very old.

The burnet roses and lilacs are fragrant, their bushes trimmed carefully into decorative groups against the southern edge of the garden. Father knows how to do everything, and his rough hands don't match his fancy clothes. He built this two-storey house with its tall, gothic windows; he tended the garden. The house's mansard roof slopes down like an elephant's brow and protects our little world. The northern edge of the garden is planted with sacred trees, whose silver-blue shadows conceal us from passers-by. Linden trees grow along the southern edge, where the veranda and large patio are. Beds of wintergreen stretch out from the foot of the patio steps like snail shells unfurling.

Mother has taken me into her lap; her warm breath on the back of my head, my hair adorned with countless silk ribbons. It's a June evening; a yellow butterfly flits past, green shadows move along the rhododendron bushes, the tablecloth is incredibly white. I can't keep my eyes open. I want to go to my room, but we're expecting guests.

Then we finally hear the whistle from a steamboat, which means they're disembarking the *Pracise*. The boat has been travelling between Riga and Ķīšezers since 1868. It's a ten-minute trip to our house through the Kaiserwald Forest – the lungs of Riga.

I think about how, on Sundays, when Father and I go sailing on the yacht – because Father is also an honorary member of the Kaiserwald Club – he doesn't seem old to me at all.

★

I don't want to talk about myself. I'm not used to it. What I can say is that I'm 30 years old, I'm quiet, reserved. I work as a nurse in a polyclinic. I don't really have any girlfriends, unless you count my hairdresser, my gynaecologist, and my tailor, all of whom I see according to a strict schedule: the hairdresser – 24 times a year; the gynaecologist – four times; the tailor – two times. So I'm social 30 days out of 365. The dentists won't be my girlfriends because I make sure the patients don't leave any gifts or under-the-table payments for them in the office. I'm of average height. Blonde. My weight is average, as is my shoe size. I'm single. I have a three-year-old Dachshund named Fil. He helps me cope with my quiet lifestyle. My mother lives out in the country. She's a widow. And that's all.

*

They've finally arrived – Father's friends and colleagues. Georg Kufalts, Juris Veibērs, two young women with narrow waists and wide hats, the director of the city zoo, Mr Grēve, with his wife and their little boy Hans. We sit around the white table; the conversations are incredibly loud, they talk about the forest, gardens, the wooden school, the flower clock, animal upkeep and appropriate conditions, about money, more money, and about the Kaiserwald. Mother passes around food and smiles to herself. Her mind is always somewhere else. I wonder what Father would say about that. Everyone is speaking German, drinking wine, eating pastries. The men's faces are energetic and serious; the women's faces kind and beautiful. I ache from how badly I want to be grown up. Later, Father lights the Japanese lanterns and puts a record on. He and mother slip into the darkness of the garden.

    Little Hans is sitting next to me. We eat marzipan sweets and feel like best friends. When Hans' parents also leave to

dance, he and I leave the table, hand in hand, and walk out
the gate. The scent of reeds and calamus wafts up from the
lake; there's the sound of frogs croaking, the new reindeer at
the zoo lowing. We run away from the noise of the dinner
party and the grown-ups' merriment. Hans is timid and
weak, but he keeps up with me. He too is only four years old.
The dusk thickens in dewy swaths, but we're not at all scared.
A little while later we realise we're standing in front of some
fresh graves. We're lost. My white socks are dirty, and my
shoelaces are untied. Hans is cold but doesn't complain. A
moment later though, he says he's scared his father will get
mad, that we have to go back. I'm scared of Mr Grēve, too,
because he's the director, but I don't know which way we're
supposed to go. I'm hungry. Hans holds back his tears, but
then his chin starts to tremble, and I break down too. We
wander off and hope for the best – tired, terrified and slightly
older. The doors to the chapel are closed. We sit on the steps
and wait. A half hour goes by, then an hour, the darkness
closes in on us and tries to separate us. Hans clings to me,
trembling. Whimpering, we get to our feet and keep walking.
Some more time passes before we finally hear shouts. We
shout back with all our strength. We run in the wrong
direction. They eventually find us. Father in just his shirt, his
forehead glistening, his hair wild; he scoops me up, smooths
my hair, showers me with kisses and hugs me, whispers my
name over and over – *Berta, Berta, Berta*. I'm cold and crying.

My mother is standing on the terrace. Her cheeks are wet
and her long hair spills unkempt down her back. She looks at
my father with strange, wide eyes, and says nothing. Back
inside, she pulls me into her arms and rocks me. I calm down.
Mother's breath smells like coffee and chocolate. I hug her
neck as hard as I can and whisper *Mamma*. Father comes in
with a cup of hot milk and sits next to us. He's seen our
visitors off, and now embraces both of us with his strong arms.

Mother rests her head on his shoulder, and we all sit still like that for a while. Then I fall asleep.

★

I didn't have a heart-wrenching or interesting childhood. Both of my little sisters died before they turned one. My father was an alcoholic and died when I was ten. When he was drunk, he'd call me a waxwing and carry me on his shoulders through the town. My mother would cry with fear, but he pretended not to notice. Once we tumbled into a ditch and I split my forehead open – I still have a small scar, here, above my eyebrows. When my father was sober, he and my mother would go for walks arm in arm and sing. I hated the countryside then and I hate it now. I never found the smell of manure to be comforting. The grunting of animals you'd just end up eating, and the hypocrisy of taking care of them? No, that's not my thing. Garden parties and peeing in bushes were also never my style. My childhood was like a short bout of diarrhoea. Sorry. Whereas in the city, I disappear, I don't get in anyone's way, no one notices me, I'm left alone. I can go to the theatre, to the movies, drink coffee by myself, do my job well and in peace. Yes, I've dated men. A few. Two, to be exact. Number one ushered me quickly but lovingly into the world of womanhood back when I was in nursing school, where all sorts of things went on in the dormitories, but number two... Number two is number two. Don't poke around where you're not wanted. Yes, a dentist! So what? What's it to you? I'm 30 years old. So there.

★

I'm eight years old when Mother and I return from Russia to our Westside Garden. Father is dead. My parents' friends are scattered. As soon as the war started, Mr Kufalts was thrown in jail, and deported to Germany a year later; Mr Weber was killed, his family stayed in Russia. What about Hans Grēve? I don't know anything about Hans.

Mother and I sit on the terrace drinking tea. Yellow-black smoke billows up from the corner of the garden. The pile of leaves Mother is burning includes Father's shirts, pants, socks and shoes, even his Sunday suit. She doesn't hear me. Mother is thin, her hair is darker and her eyes colder. She's staring off into the distance. Not even her eyelashes move, and I feel useless.

It's 11 o'clock at night when I bring a blanket out to her. She sits like that for another hour.

When she comes in later to tuck me in, I panic and clutch my pillow to my chest with both arms. I've hidden Father's white bowtie in it. I don't understand Mother.

In the morning, the garden and the wind both smell like charred wool.

Then we dig, fertilise, rake, plant, cut, saw, weed and sow. The two of us blackened with soil.

*

He gave me Fil. In his place. To remember him by. And to protect me. That's the only thing I haven't said yet.

*

It's 1933. I'm now Mrs Pempere. I have a rosy-violet evening gown and silk shoes; I am 56 kilograms of devastating sex-appeal. Ernests keeps an eye on me like a watchdog that has a mean bark. He's a little like my father. Quick and strong. I'll never know everything about him. Ernests is Andrejs Zeidaks' right-hand man, a landscape designer. Zeidaks has replaced

Kufalts, and criticises his teacher for his dense greenery and damp shaded areas, for the complicated web of pathways and his choice of flowers. He and Ernests blaze through the Ziedonis, Latgale and Vērmane Gardens, the Brothers and Rainis Cemeteries. Rose gardens, colour coordination, contrasting leaves, summer theatres and outdoor seating, roads and the gardens of the future.

The Westside Garden is blooming and growing, too. Ernests has installed a fountain among the lindens – a bronze statuette with a round face. It reminds me of Hans. In the afternoons, Mother and I sit on the terrace; the honeysuckle is fragrant, the water splashes, and we wait for Ernests to come home.

My husband and I go to the restaurant Mona, for dinner on Saturdays, often just eating in the Gambia Room. Sunday nights we always have guests over. Like my parents once did, we too light the Japanese lanterns, put a record on. But we have more wine. My friends from the Academy of Art, Ellija and Nora, come wearing wide, black slacks and berets; the Streif brothers come, owners of our favourite coffee shop, famous for their special blends; the director of the canning factory, Mr Krevalds, comes too, and brings us freshly-canned pickles and sprats; Ernests' landscaping colleagues bring their families; and I am young. Mother grimaces and calls us civilians. Her gaze starts to wander off into the distance, but she manages to heatedly curse all governments, all men in power and all their servants. Mother loves Ernests, and they both die eight years later. Far away from Westside Garden, where I remain alone with four-year-old Marija.

We both sit on the terrace, wrapped in shawls, our lips trembling; the fountain has rusted over, and I am old. Just as old as you are today, Veronika.

Mežaparks is in shambles; now and then, men in various uniforms crawl out of the woods like fleas and wander past the house. The flowerbeds are overgrown; I don't get up, I sit, I rock Marija and breathe into her light, soft hair.

★

My room is 6m² – we just managed to fit the old couch, a small vanity, and a bookcase into it. One of the doors in the room leads to a three-season porch, and the other door leads to the kitchen, where everyone who lives here prepares their food: Mrs Pempere, Old Oto, Mrs Ozers and the upstairs neighbours, Ļusja and Vlad and their six-year-old daughters Ira and Taņa.

From early spring and well into autumn, Mrs Pempere carries monsteras, rhododendrons, leopard lilies, jade plants, aloe, dracaenas, billgergias, myrtle, grape ivy and cast-iron plant out onto the veranda, sets them on the windowsills, on stands of various heights and little tables. This is where I spend most of my summers, among the flower pots, sitting next to the oval tea table and reading. I wipe the dust off the plants' leaves twice a week. Mrs Pempere comes out to me in the afternoons with a blue coffee pot, and we talk about women's ideals in the past and present. Fil sleeps on my slippers and snores. It's been three years since I first rented a room from the old woman. The house is full of albums, letters, diaries, yellowed magazines and records. On weekdays, at 2pm, Mrs Pempere brings Fil an earthenware bowl of soup, which the dog happily eats once he's left by himself.

The so-called Westside Garden is divided into four sections. Mrs Pempere owns the half with the terrace; she's 80 years old, but still takes care of it until her face is beet red and she has to go lie down. On Ļusja's side, where the sacred trees are growing, the flowerbeds have been razed and asphalted. On Mrs Pempere's side, the basin of the rusted fountain still has sand in it from when Ira and Taņa used it as their childhood sandbox. Now both girls are grown up; they spend their evenings at the parties in Mežaparks while Ļusja nervously walks up and down Mārburga Street waiting for them to come home. Ļusja hangs laundry above the rose beds between the linden trees, even though that's Mrs Pempere's side. Vlad works in construction; it's dirty work, which is why the line is full of laundry twice a week. There's nowhere else to tie up the line. It's a poorly designed garden. When Ira and Taņa were born, Ļusja had planted two poplars – but once the girls were older the trees had to be chopped down because they were allergic to the trees' fuzz. That's why the clothesline had to go between the lindens.

Mrs Ozers is a 70-year-old widow. When Colonel Ozers was still alive, no one had to worry about the maintenance or repairs. A group of soldiers would arrive, slap a coat of brownish-green paint on the house, spread gravel to even out the paths, and everything was fixed. But now, Mrs Pempere's part of the house was painted green, while the second story and the right wing of the first story were pink. Mrs Pempere had no say in the matter. She also had no say in the matter when Ļusja and Vlad put up a gazebo in the garden. She shouted and cried, but Ļusja only stuck her tongue out at the old woman, a reminder that the time of the bourgeois had ended. Vlad painted the fence pink, too, but he hasn't nailed the gate together yet or screwed the hinges in all the way. The gate rattles and bangs in the wind, and at night it sounds like people are coming and going through it and wandering the garden.

Old Oto is no spring chicken, either. He's 76. He's a divorcé and loves flowers. Of course, Ļusja stripped him of his portion of the garden, but he has four flowerbeds next to the gate all to himself. They're lush with phloxes, pansies, poppies and dahlias. Mrs Pempere is appalled by this combination, but she won't say so out loud. Old Oto will at least watch Latvian television programmes with her.

41

But I like it here. Mrs Pempere is a complicated person, but I get along well with her. She leaves me alone, and I live my own life.

★

I know, Veronika, you secretly want me to write you in. Why else would you be so polite and diligent? You don't have an easy life, I can see that. You're nice, quiet, know how to cook and bake, and you've probably learned everything there is to know about childcare; you dress well and don't fool around with slacks and bobbed haircuts, but act like a real woman. A dog isn't just a toy to you, you're responsible. You even treat the neighbours well. Better than I do. But something smoulders in you, and it makes me sad. And what if my Marija ever comes back? I can't, Veronika.

People walk about, banging the gate behind them. They sit and chat, their fleshy behinds hanging over the faded walls of the gazebo, drink tea from a thermos with scarves on their heads. Where is the warm light in the shade of the linden?

Veronika, he's waiting for you. You'll disappear for an hour again. It's a good thing. I'm keeping my fingers crossed. Mrs Ozers said he's an upstanding gentleman. He wears a long trench-coat and smokes a cigar. I won't go to bed until you come home. My heart is restless, but you won't see that.

★

I've found one. A husband. Three weeks straight of ringing at the gate at 9pm. Herbert. A pale, pathetic lab tech from the Institute of Biology. Tortured, deep-set eyes with immobile pupils the size of pinpricks. I've been sitting with him at the clinic for half an hour. He fainted after they pulled one of his teeth. When he came to, he said to me: 'Now you know everything there is about me.' *Well, well*, I had thought, and looked away. The next day he was there with daffodils. Not smiling though, because it was one of his front teeth they'd pulled. And now we're walking through the forest. I laugh, smile; he says nothing, takes me by the elbow now and then. He stares at me when he thinks I'm not looking. He trips. Sometimes he tries to kiss me, but then Fil barks wildly, jumps up on Herbert, and I don't do anything to stop him. It's a little uncomfortable. Everything with him is a little uncomfortable. His pale, long tongue right in front of me. Herbert wants to come over for tea, and I know why, but I don't let him. I tell him my landlady is prudish. We walk night after night until I catch pneumonia. Then he shows up – attentive, concerned, with stewed fruit and chocolate. Mrs Pempere doesn't even come out of her room; the whole house is silent. They're all putting themselves in my shoes. I absolutely hate it. Even Old Oto has locked himself in his room and won't go out to use the toilet. Herbert makes coffee in the kitchen, tucks in my blanket and caresses my forehead. Fil growls threateningly from under the sofa. Day after day, for three whole weeks. When I fall asleep, or rather when Herbert thinks I'm asleep, he slides a hand under the blanket and, with a sad whimper, gropes me. I grit my teeth and let it happen as I feign sleep. There's something about it I don't like.

*

He's amazing, Veronika! He loves you, believe me. You've changed, too, you've grown nervous and snippy. You jump at the slightest sound and always look angry. You tease him by showering Fil with kisses. Why do you wait until Herbert is over to call Fil sweet things like little dove, my pet, chickadee, darling? The dog is mean to Herbert. I once saw him lift his leg and piss on Herbert's trousers, and how he growls and whines when Herbert comes over.

The bins reek; there's no wind this spring. The terrace steps are crumbling, we should have someone come out with a bag of cement. The seagulls have defecated over every surface. Do you feel that sharp, sickly-sweet stench clinging to the air, coming from the direction of the lake? There's no wind, but you can smell it all the way to here. Let's go, Veronika, let's take a walk through the cemetery some morning, all right? I don't like doing it alone anymore. I don't like a lot of things anymore.

★

He makes my skin crawl. When Herbert is next to me I think about death. Everything feels hopeless, filled with darkness and heavy. When he's over, the reindeer in the zoo always start to go crazy. I can't fall asleep after he leaves. We struggle. Quietly. He undresses me slowly, almost lazily. He doesn't turn the light on, feels around as if he's blind. How could you like being blind? Each time Herbert presses me up against the heater I get burned, because Mrs Pempere runs the heat in the summer, too, she's always cold. I can't cry out; her room is right next door and I'm embarrassed. My fingers rake through Herbert's smooth, black hair; he's panting in excitement. Fil is locked out on the veranda, sniffing and sneezing. When it's over, I let the dog back in and he barks at Herbert. Then I take Fil into my lap, pet him, he licks my face and calms down. Herbert is quiet and watches me for a long time. Two days later he's back. He's brought medicine for Mrs Pempere and aster seeds from West Germany. Herbert doesn't criticise me, just studies me, like the white rats in his laboratory.

When we walk through the forest and I break out of those four walls, I hear Herbert muttering to himself *Bombycilla gurrulus gurrulus.* 'What's that,' I ask, but he just kisses me, kisses me, kisses me. Everything in me trembles, I'm debilitated. I mix up medications, forget to sterilise the instruments.

In the cemetery, Herbert reads the names of the deceased out loud; we sit on a bench by the headstones and stare at the clouds, but I'm anxious the entire time. I'm afraid. *Bombycilla gurrulus gurrulus.*

★

Ira is pregnant. There's a commotion upstairs. Vlad is yelling and hitting his daughter. Ļusja is sitting in the kitchen, crying. The strong scent of camphor wafts from Old Oto's room; he has joint pain. It's Mrs Ozers' birthday; she's invited everyone to the gazebo for grog and sandwiches. Her son has brought supplies from the veterans' store. You should come too, Veronika, and bring Herbert. We'll have a drink and chat. I could've offered up my terrace for her to use, but she didn't ask… I got Vlad and Ira calmed down. 'That's the way it goes,' I told him. And he goes: 'Where are they going to live?!' 'With you, Pempere?' 'Huh?!' Vlad laughed at me, as if I were the pregnant one, but then he stopped. I made them wash their faces and gather their wits, now we're all sitting together. The samovar is steaming; Mrs Ozers has a new fringed shawl, and we raise our glasses to those who have fallen in the war. Veronika sits there like a stuffed bird, her eyes immobile, but Herbert is lively, talkative and attentive. Ļusja and Taņa are singing some love song, I can't handle it, but I have to. It's Mrs Ozers' birthday, after all. Old Oto is staring dreamily at the leaves and looks asleep. Mrs Ozers taps the back of my hand, like a gesture to calm me, and invites me to drink. After a second drink, at 80 years old, I can't do a third, so I laugh and push her hand away. Do they all think old people are fools? I see it in every glance. Veronika is convinced that I understand nothing about sensitive situations. But I do. She's adapting. And Herbert will get through it. Except Fil is making things difficult. When the two of them go out together, the dog leaves a horrid present for them in the centre of the sofa. But Herbert says nothing. He doesn't speak, just acts. He trims the dead branches from the bushes, brings fertiliser for the roses. You can depend on him. But Veronika's mind is always off somewhere. Spiteful thing. I know that look.

★

The two of us are lying by the lake. We've left Fil at home. Mrs Pempere said she'd feed him. Herbert is so tan and smooth, he's actually a tantalising specimen. I press my nose against his shoulder; it's hot. We can't swim because the water is dirty. The grass is littered with corks, lids from cans and empty Sever cigarette packets. Flies everywhere. Herbert lies still.

Volumes shift, lines tremble, the air is rosy. The flowers on the terrace wilt; Mrs Pempere, her mother and Marija are sitting outside. The rustling of silk, the scent of pines. Their profiles waver like colourful ruffles against the red wall of Virginia creepers, the vines vibrate, hair slips, tangles, unravels, unfurls in seashell-curls. I draw nearer, but don't make it there. I pull away. Farther away with each step I take closer. I slide into a green, cool, thick mass, dewy grass, smooth sand, I shrink, I'm small, frozen and I don't know the way home. The chapel doors are closed, I run, the sand flies. The waxwings with their reddish-grey backs peck at juniper berries, their crops tremble as they turn their heads, the carmine-red spots on their wings glimmer, the bright yellow of their tails flashes. Someone whispers – *'Bombycilla gurrulus gurrulus.'* I shout: 'Hey, where are you, come here,' but the echo sounds farther and farther away: '*Ulus, ulus*. My little waxwing!'

There she stands – Berta – in her white socks, countless silk ribbons in her braids, watching me thoughtfully. She curtsies and extends her hand. Berta Pempere. I nod; red waxwings shoot up into the sky, and we hug. 'Ah, you're four, too!' 'Of course I am. But where's Hans Grēve? We have to be on board the *Pracise* in three minutes.' 'No, Marija got on a different boat.' We walk off hand in hand until dusk separates us.

Herbert has untied my swimsuit and is caressing my breasts. I sit up abruptly and shove him away, harder than I mean to. Herbert purses his lips and asks through gritted teeth what my problem is. I say I have a nervous disorder and, maybe, even syphilis. Nobody is around, so he picks me up and carries me home. I don't want to object.

*

Mrs Pempere died half an hour ago. In her rocking chair out on the terrace – facing the rose beds. Ļusja is bawling and caressing her grey, curly hair. Mrs Ozers stands completely still, rapidly blinking her eyes. Old Oto is crying. Ira and Taņa have gone to a friend's house. Vlad is at work. The garden gate squeaks and rattles. People come and go. Herbert holds me. After a moment I realise it's Fil who is howling from the veranda. I pull him towards me, pet him, murmur something to him through my tears, but he just pees on my dress. I put him down and he runs over to Mrs Pempere. He sniffs her, whimpers, sniffs her again and lies down on top of her white summer sandals.

We want to bring her inside, but Fil glares at Herbert from under his lashes, and won't let us get near her; his teeth are bared as he growls. It seems I was right. Herbert says: 'Bowlegged shit.'

Then I break up with him. Right there. In front of everyone. Even Mrs Pempere.

★

She hasn't even been buried yet, when I find Fil on the sofa in my room. Motionless, small, his throat slit. A dark puddle coagulates on the green silk rug. Old Oto comes bursting into my room. His dentures clattering and his voice catching, he whispers that a strange man had come in here. My colleague.

★

Fil and Mrs Pempere have been buried. Separately, of course. I sit on the terrace and wait. It's as if the house has been scared into silence. I hear the light sound of dripping water. I look up. The fountain is working again. Hans Grēve sputters out yellow, rusty water, and it disappears into the grey sand. Finally I feel familiar, slow hands on me, and I close my eyes.

Killing Mrs Cecilia Bochs

Arno Jundze

Translated by Kaija Straumanis

No, no, Doctor, you didn't hear wrong... I honestly came to the conclusion that the only way to achieve total well-being was to *kill* the kind, old, and all-round harmless Mrs Cecilia Bochs. Because there was no way this elderly woman, who at that time was pushing 80, was going to kick the bucket on her own.

You think I'm crazy?

Or maybe you'll say that, these days, one has to wipe out at least half a dozen tiny, feeble old ladies to be able to afford a respectable meal at a fancy restaurant? A little joke à la Raskolnikov – with a bit of axe and borscht on the side.

I'm telling you, Doctor – it all depends on the situation. Someone else might have worked up quite a sweat with all the old ladies they murder, but I would've been content with just Cecilia Bochs.

Oh, hang on. I forgot to introduce myself! My name is Augustus Bochs, sole heir of the proprietor, Cecilia Bochs. That should explain a lot vis-à-vis this murder business. I understand I'm supposed to spend our first session telling you about myself:

I'm 47 years old and, as you can see, I'm short, thickset, partially bald – although I take great care to hide this with a comb over – and I have love handles. I'm near-sighted and I never married. I wanted to, once, but it didn't work out. It was a long time ago, in the Andropov era. She ended up going with a wealthy warehouse director who owned a Lada Samara and a summerhouse in Saulkrasti. I'll tell it like it is; women don't look twice at guys like me. They love rich, lean macho-men who have a Marlboro between their lips and a fat wallet. It's not worth pretending I don't fall into that category. The largest amount of money I've ever had, to date, in my tattered wallet is 250 lats. I'd found it, believe it or not, lying on the street. I was just walking along, saw it, and picked it up. It had probably fallen out of some rich guy's pocket, or maybe he'd just thrown it down in front of some girls to show off how rich he was. It was by that restaurant, Sēnītes. You remember that hooligan hangout, where mobsters were gunned down now and then in downtown Riga, right by Ģertrūde Church? Back then all the bigwigs hung out there, and there were murders and explosions... All the newspapers wrote about it.

I forgot to say – I'm an engineering contractor by trade, something no one needs. Graduated 1977 from the Arvīds Pelše Riga Technical University. My first job, if you don't count the three years I spent in the army corps of engineers, was at VEF, Soviet Latvia's legendary industrial flagship. I was a junior in the construction department. I made 110 roubles a month. Later, I was in the construction business and made 225 roubles. And so it continued, until the Awakening. Everything gave way, crumbled, fell apart. In the end my own firm went under. I was unemployed. When my late mother found out, may she rest in peace, she cried. 'We Bochs, we're such hardworking people, but you're just a maggot, you disgust me. What are you good for anyway?'

And you know, my mother was right. I really am a complete failure. It's awful to admit it, but it's the truth. While others were privatising, stealing, cheating and making money,

I stood by and watched and was as honest as a saint. Only dumber... much dumber.

What happened after that... it makes me sick to even think about it. After she passed, I first took a job as a guard, then as a soldier, then briefly even a job in a morgue. We all need to eat, and I had to make rent somehow! Meanwhile everyone else is making millions, buying Mercedes, taking trips abroad, but I'm scrounging for cigarette butts just to get a smoke... pretty pathetic, right?

Yes, Doctor, for you to better understand why, in order to achieve total well-being, I needed in all seriousness to make a decision on whether or not to kill Mrs Cecilia Bochs – like in those boring stories by Latvian authors – you have to look at my family history.

No, no, Doctor, don't worry! I'll try not to waste your precious time by going through my entire family tree, starting with Adam, or going into the numerous stories from the personal lives of a German baron and a Latvian maid. I'll just say that my grandfather, Benedict Bochs, was a wealthy butcher shop owner back in the day. He'd been groomed to be a landlord, and up until the Revolution had managed enormous properties somewhere in far-away Samara. When the First World War was over, and the communists came to power in Russia, he quickly realised that he wouldn't be able to live under Lenin and, together with my grandmother, they decided to return to Latvia. Miraculously, Grandfather managed to circumvent Russian marauders as well as the Red Army's border guards, who weren't much better than the marauders. All their assets had been converted – with great foresight before things fell apart – into golden ten rouble coins; Benedict Bochs hid the coins in their iron bedposts, the heels of boots and other unlikely places, but not without stashing a pouch filled with a couple of gold and silver coins and worthless trinkets at the bottom of a saddlebag to throw them off.

Grandfather's calculations were spot-on! The pouch, along with the entire saddlebag, their silver spoons, and their Meissen porcelain were confiscated by the greedy Russians. They also managed to beat a bit around my grandmother Elizabeth Bochs' bush, so to speak, but in this time of post-Revolution chaos, all civilians could do was look away, or else get a knife to the gut. What was important, though, is that they managed to get to Latvia with gold. A lot of gold. Enough to buy a solid piece of land with a wooden house on this end of Tērbatas Street, and to open their first shop. Old Bochs was a truly resourceful man and knew that it would be crazy to work with trivial things in the new republic – when times get tough, people think first and foremost about food. The idea for a butcher's shop was just as smart as the trick with the gold hidden in the bedposts because, believe it or not, by the beginning of 1940 Benedict Bochs had four shops throughout Riga, three booths at the Central Market and two brick buildings he rented out, also on Tērbatas Street. I should mention that my grandmother was a strong woman, and after the horrible experience with the Russian border guards, once they'd returned to their fatherland, she soon bounced back – it was lucky the Reds didn't stick her with some disease or other – and in 1923 she gave birth to Benedict Bochs' first heiress. Two years later my mother, Genoveva Bochs, was joined by a little sister, Cecilia.

Unlike the rather complicated turn of events depicted in the newspapers these days, the fate of my family was simple to the point of being banal. In 1940, the communists threw Benedict Bochs in the Central Prison where they shot him so they wouldn't have to ship him off to Siberia; the butcher's and rental properties were nationalised. During German rule, Elizabete Bochs ran the household with her two daughters, who were of marrying age by that point. The youngest, Cecilia, proved to be more skilled in this department, and in

1943 (at barely 18 years old) dragged to the altar a man who, as my mother ironically observed, was a purebred stallion: a blond SS officer – a Latvian from Kurzeme, to boot, who together with the infamous Kārlis Arajs Kommando had been stationed in Rumbula Forest. Needless to say, when the Russians resumed power, Cecilia and her SS-man headed for the hills. Somewhere along the way to Silesia the train they were on was bombed and the blond stallion died on the spot. A direct hit, so to speak. But poor Cecilia went into premature labour right there next to the burning railway carriages. She lost the baby, and the traumatised Cecilia was barren after that. Which was a lucky break for me.

The elder sister, Genoveva Bochs, stayed in Latvia during those turbulent times. Of course, she and my grandmother stuffed their valuables with other valuables and had plans to board a ship sailing far away from here when, at the last second, Grandmother had a stroke. She suffered for a week before heading off to greener pastures. During that time the communists had again taken control of Riga, and there was nowhere left to run. My mother kept her wits about her in those difficult times. Once she had an understanding of her situation, Genoveva Bochs quickly landed herself a stocky KGB major (I'm apparently his spitting image). They never got married because the major already had a wife somewhere in Russia, but my mother's relationship with a man from the KGB saved her from deportation, and even got her a job in a national trade company as a goods manager – a position which at that time was worth its weight in gold.

Stalin died in 1953, and Mother's boyfriend was soon assigned back to work in Moscow. You could say that he simply went back to his Russian wife. I was born in 1954. In 1989, my mother also suffered a stroke. The doctors ruled it was a myocardial infarction. She died in the ambulance on the way to the hospital. I was alone. I'll be honest with you, it was incredibly unpleasant because, even up until her final moments, Mother had been the one who had managed the household: she had waited in those long queues and had been the one to prepare our meals. And I – a good for nothing bachelor – was up to my ears in trouble… Everything was crumbling and falling apart! I bumbled along through life somehow, but I'll be honest, there were occasions when I was just a few minutes from climbing out through the attic to hang myself next to the neighbours' bed linens. I guess what got to me the most was that I was a total zero, a failure, a fool. All around me were these fancy restaurants, casinos, rich peoples' cars, all these shiny objects that any self-respecting Soviet citizen hadn't even dreamed of in 50 years, and then there's you, a real pauper with not even enough change in your pocket for a beer. It would've made sense had I been an alcoholic, a total idiot, sick or even mentally disabled. But no, Doctor! I was a normal guy, an engineer with the highest education. And a really good engineer at that! But, and pardon my French, an engineer up to his ears in shit.

I don't know how that all would have ended, but then the country regained its independence and they announced the denationalisation of properties. Can you imagine a greater gift from above to a failure like me? Two rental properties, practically in downtown Riga! (The third one had burned down after the war.) What more could a guy want? And my mother had had some foresight and saved all of our old family documents, including birth and death certificates, which would prove my right to the properties. And then, just when I had almost decided that I would sell off one of the buildings and use the money to live the high life with some long-legged blondes, this old witch showed up. Straight from Toronto! Well, with a layover in Copenhagen, of course.

Almost 40 years without so much as a letter, and then, she gets a whiff of cash, and is suddenly right there like some kind of leech! A true representative of the Bochs bloodline! I should have pushed that old bat straight into the lift shaft. At first though, she seemed as harmless as a cloud; greying, slight, all smiles. She wanted to come back, to renovate her father's place. She was willing to sell her villa in faraway Canada, and use her life savings, which weren't insignificant. As the sole heir after her, I would get everything later on: both her as well as the rest of the Bochs family properties. But in that moment, I had nothing. What was I going to do with those big properties without a cent to my name? You had to spend money to make money, and any idiot could just sell the buildings. That money would just melt away like last year's snow! And that's how I would learn one day that the entirety of the Bochs' property was divided up into little parcels, and all I would end up with were the worthless attic and basement.

I have to admit, the old lady was talking so reasonably, sweet as honey; the devil himself must have scrambled my brains. I honestly started to believe that the buildings were in disrepair, with rusted roofs and often full of, pardon my French, piss-soaked stairwells, communal cockroach nests and nightmare tenants. Of course, you would have to spend money on the buildings in order to make money. And, needless to say Doctor, Cecilia Bochs persuaded me. She opened her wallet (which really was quite thick) and reclaimed the properties in literally just a few months. You see, if you can make the council members happy with a few little gifts, then things move ahead rather quickly. When the buildings and land were reclaimed, we went to a notary and, true to her word, Cecilia Bochs bequeathed all her Latvian and Canadian properties to me, and I was officially named manager of her estate. So far so good, but that was only the beginning...

The trouble started in my first month of managing the first building, when I learned that the old woman was actually a thrifty little bitch! No, it wasn't like she lived off of trash and walked around in rags; it was the opposite, this woman knew about fashion, and never ordered a bottle of wine cheaper than 10 lats. Meanwhile I had to account for every santim I spent. What's more, the old woman had absolutely no clue about the Latvian tax system. Remember that romantic period in the mid-1920s? Now, it's total anarchy and the illusions of the respectable businessman are crashing down, Doctor! The banks rob you without so much as batting an eye, and then those banks just go bankrupt. When you need something done by an expert, a handyman, a bin man – there's no receipt, no cheque! If you want something from the local government – it takes bribe upon bribe! Then a tax inspector shows up at the end of the year – a guy dumb as a rock – and starts doing your taxes as if none of these criminal bankers ever existed, but also as if you hadn't put a single santim into your property! Signs from God! And then there's the receipt for the bookkeeping! Cheques for this and that. Meanwhile my aunt is buying building materials and can't even remember where she got them from… Just try and pull all those ends together so the tax inspector doesn't bring you to court at the end of the year. What's more, if something isn't the way she wants it, Cecilia Bochs gets angry, and the worthless building manager is to blame for everything.

You see, Doctor, if you were a salaried employee in some company, you could just bid them good day and leave! But what am I supposed to do – a legal heir? I couldn't even tell the old bat to go to hell! Otherwise, God forbid, Mrs Bochs will change her mind, change her will and bequeath all her belongings to the University of Latvia or some animal shelter. Don't laugh, Doctor, I'm serious!

Cecilia Bochs also had a very strange sense of compassion. Believe it or not, every day she'd buy at least a couple kilos of those expensive Lido sausages and feed them to the mangy cats that live in bins. Just imagine, an elderly lady in an elegant

Sears coat and fancy Gucci shoes feeding street cats! I'd happily shoot those miserable creatures dead. Once, we were in a cab and she started to scream hysterically because she'd spotted a ragged mutt wandering along Brīvības Street. *That poor doggy – it's going to get run over!* It was so stupid – the cab driver almost crashed into a trolley out of fright! But do you think her strange sense of compassion carried over to humans? Don't hold your breath! Once, without so much as batting an eye, Cecilia Bochs sued old Ms Alma from apartment No. 5 – a 94-year-old woman who had lived through who knows how many regimes, and Siberia. She literally threw Ms Alma out onto the street, saying that if the old lady couldn't pay, she could scram! Good thing social services took pity on Ms Alma and set her up in an old folks' home, where she died from a broken heart only a week later.

Yes, the moment Cecilia Bochs' insufferable habits began to make themselves known in all their glory was after that big row and court interference, which left vacant the large Bochs' flat in the building facing the street. (In her day, my mother had taken the advice of a KGB agent and had moved to a two-bedroom flat in the building facing the courtyard.) Instead of commissioning a normal European-style remodelling with an elegant bathroom and gas heating, the backwards biddy started on about how everyone here in Latvia was a fool, and how she wouldn't permit those kinds of vulgar atrocities in the old Bochs flat. (Tiles, you see, were only put on the walls and the floors in airports and public restrooms, linoleum was the manifestation of the Germans' commonness, and a gas stove could explode!) After chasing off dozens of modern architects and designers, she found some crooked, old-world geezer with a roll of drafting paper tucked under his arm and a pencil behind his ear. Between the two of them, they created something that wouldn't be out of place at the Latvian Ethnographic Open-Air Museum. It's a good thing the fellow passed away soon after, because during construction he'd become almost a kind of adviser to Cecilia and, I swear to God, I started to worry these two idiot geriatrics would start plotting together for real.

Anyway, we were talking about the apartment... See, her mother and father had furnished and decorated that apartment, and so it was Cecilia Bochs' moral duty to preserve their memory. Alright, fine, memory, nostalgia, but goddamn it, that had been almost a hundred years ago! So tell me, why in God's name should a modern-day range be built out of pieces of porcelain – essentially a toilet bowl – and be installed on a wood-burning, potbelly stove? What's more, this range the old hag had installed for almost 1,000 lats has no hood, it just smokes, and it's no surprise because when she lived in Canada, the crone was so spoiled that she didn't even know how to plug in a microwave!

You know, Doctor, I could write a book about all her habits and peculiarities, but I couldn't object to anything she did. I tried a few times, but I knew that the slightest sign of disobedience would end with her rewriting her will, and that was not something anyone in his right mind would want to let happen. Right, Doctor? And that's how I came round to the idea of killing Mrs Cecilia Bochs.

It wasn't a spontaneous decision – like taking an axe to her skull, or something. I had to come up with something more finessed. You see, Doctor, it would be foolish to end her life in some obvious and crude way, because as the sole heir, I would fall immediately under suspicion. I could, of course, always stage a robbery or something, but Mrs Cecilia Bochs had already been mugged a couple times within the first month of her return to Latvia. Since then, the old lady had been more cautious – she didn't go out at night and didn't invite strangers into her flat. One of the first things she did after the properties had been privatised was to have keypad door locks installed in all our buildings. I also had an emergency key to her place. Obviously, there was no use entertaining thoughts of a robbery-homicide scenario; I'd have to be much more careful...

And so, Doctor, I decided to do it in a way that looked like a total accident. I'll say right now that it didn't work. I tried on three separate occasions.

I don't know – maybe God was watching over the old broad.

The first-time I tried tampering with the light switch to the basement, so when the witch came in on her daily rounds to check on the properties like some kind of taskmaster, she'd flip the light on and get electrocuted. And Jesus how I sweated while I worked – it took me forever to make it look like the switch was merely worn down from age. If you only knew what came of it. Doctor, please, don't laugh! Around three o'clock in the morning I got a panicked telephone call – the bathroom pipe in No. 47 had burst, and the neighbours below them were all but drowning! And two storeys below was a furniture store... Absolute madness! I jumped out of bed and into my slippers and raced down to the basement. It's only by the grace of God that my slippers were pool sandals with a rubber sole, otherwise I probably wouldn't be sitting here today. I was in the hospital for two weeks, and I still have scars on my right hand.

My second attempt ended no less curiously. One day I happened to notice that someone had tried to steal the cover of the manhole in the corner of the courtyard. Apparently, the cast-iron cover had proved too difficult to carry off, and the thief had left it lying crookedly over the manhole. The cover had been left on the 5m-deep shaft in a way that, if someone were to step on it, it would flip up, immediately sending the unsuspecting pedestrian down the concrete well before they could utter a peep. Anyway, Cecilia Bochs never watched where she stepped. I spent four days trying to inconspicuously coax her into the vicinity of the manhole... You have a thing all planned, all figured out, but on the fifth morning it was a local policeman who fell into the manhole! Now you see him, now you don't. Straight down, like a meteor! As if the manhole had been waiting just for him all along. The policeman broke his ankle. I suppose it was fate. But just imagine the racket that came after: accident reports, proceedings, committees, the municipal bureaucrats, the media... It was crazy.

I prepared for my third attempt particularly carefully. I'd planned everything down to a T, including my alibi and that the old woman would be found lying under a pile of collapsed construction scaffolding. But wouldn't you know, Doctor, on the morning it was all to happen, Cecilia Bochs called me and asked me in a weak voice to come to her flat because she was feeling rather unwell. On the way over I asked my neighbour from No. 16 to come with me (she works as a paramedic). And there she lay in her museum-esque flat in her museum-esque bed. Small, withered, frail, she looked me in the eyes and said: 'I think I'm dying. Forgive me if I was unkind to you.'

We rushed Cecilia Bochs to the expensive, fancy hospital, hooked her up to IVs, but it didn't help. My mother's sister joined her ancestors, and a week later it came to me to organise her funeral.

You may wonder, Doctor, what exactly is the problem here, then? In the end Cecilia Bochs died a natural death and all the formalities of the inheritance were squared away a few months ago. I'm a rich property owner and can finally afford the company of any woman I want, and to be honest, I don't feel the slightest bit guilty about having wanted to kill Mrs Cecilia Bochs...

But there is one thing that keeps nagging at me, nagging and nagging. You see, Doctor, how can I put this...

See, back when I was poor and always down on my luck, I believed that if I had money then I'd finally start to feel like a person. Now I have everything I could ever want. Everything! But that feeling didn't come, and still hasn't...

Does that make sense?

Doctor!

Deep down I still feel like the worthless maggot my late mother said I was, a man who couldn't even manage to kill a helpless old lady.

But I guess that's not something medicine can fix, right?

Wonderful New Latvia

Ilze Jansone

Translated by Suzanne McQuade

THE TRAM ARRIVED ALMOST soundlessly, and Katrīna, settling in by the window, flipped through the magazine she'd bought at the kiosk. Nothing caught her eye. Come to think of it, she wasn't really sure why she'd bought it in the first place; she could have just borrowed it from work. But dragging herself to the thirteenth floor just for a magazine – which didn't have anything worth reading in it anyway – seemed like a lot of effort. None of the library visitors bothered either, as few as there were. Mostly they came to use the database and occasionally the internet. There were usually about three or four of them sitting in the reading room, hunched over their keyboards. Not like it used to be, when people would sign up for books even when there was a long waiting list.

Katrīna knew well how people once read books in libraries. The profession was her birthright and a source of pride; at least one librarian in every generation. Grandma would tell of how the country folk celebrated Sundays by checking books out of the library as a treat to read after a leisurely breakfast. She made an effort to read all of the books, any she came across, and she knew the contents of them all (and trust me, she knew what was inside every reader, too, and could easily find the right reader for any book).

The tram was almost empty, so she could sit where she wanted. The next stop was T/C Iesalkāja so there was still quite a way to go before she reached work. The No. 18 bus had only started running rather recently and was, for the time being, the only bus that went along the Southern Bridge instead of the Stone Bridge.

Just over the Stone Bridge, there was a beautiful building where Mama's father had worked as a bank teller when he was younger. 'He met your grandma right there in that building,' Mama said. When she'd read that they were going to be renovating it, she made a special trip to take a picture of the building, and it was a good thing she did: the renovation was, in reality, a demolition, and the relocation was a liquidation. 'Good thing Papa never saw this,' Mama cried as she developed the film. She exhibited her photographs here and there, graduated from the art academy, having studied photography, but mostly everyone smirked at her: 'What are you trying to do with your pictures, sweetheart? You need to spend more time studying, master filming and editing, work on some detective series, then come back and we'll talk.'

Mama was offended, no one appreciated real art in this banana republic, so she turned on her heel and left for Ireland. She worked for a few years as a cleaner, called home every so often and cried. *To hell with it*, she thought, *home is neither here nor there*. But gradually she got used to it.

Mama knew that the only way you could take the past with you was through photographs, and so she organised a solo exhibition of her work. And, as it turned out, her photographs made their way into the hearts and minds of the people there – as well as onto book jackets, walls, posters, CDs and websites. She received job offers, photographed ad campaigns, and became a real success. You wouldn't recognise her now, she walks around beaming, living another life. When they ask her about her homeland, she becomes gloomy and says if only she could have taken those beautiful views with her, that countryside and forest, those filigree buildings... But in truth, they were all safeguarded for her in pictures; there's nothing left of it back home, just ultramodern buildings and smog. So gradually she learned to love Ireland's countryside, travelling now and again, taking more photographs. Katrīna still invited her to come for a visit; *Come back, see your native city*, but Mama said no, she had enough grey hairs, she was done, she'd never set foot in this country again, better to remember it the way it had been. Mama didn't handle change well. What could you do? The important thing is that she can live her own life, flying off to India for a holiday! She should be back in two days; Katrīna must catch her on Skype one night so she can hear all about how things are going with her photographs.

They had started to build Katrīna's current workplace in the plot where the torn-down buildings once stood, but, as soon as the old buildings were demolished, those in charge reconsidered. It was a shame to allocate such valuable real estate – practically right in the centre of town – to something like the 'Castle of Light,' even if it was a national icon. They even conducted a national poll: 99.5 per cent voted that it would be better to have office space in such a great neighbourhood. Here, it's always been customary to do what the nation wants, and so they decided to modify the plans, and the new design would include office space inside the Castle of Light. They even formed a special committee – the cream of the crop – and announced another design competition.

Katrīna's cousin Armands, an architect, whipped up a design like no other. He planned to refurbish the old factory buildings right there along the edge of the Daugava and install a beautiful tin roof that would reflect the light beautifully. There would be an underground car park, no plastic or plasterboard, all wood, brick and glass, and a small park next to it with benches all around; and inside, a fountain to maintain the correct humidity. He'd researched all the minute details of the latest technologies for book preservation, temperature and air humidity. Katrīna helped him retrieve information from the right websites; she was a librarian after all, she knew the internet like the back of her hand and researching new information was a doddle for her. Armands was an experienced architect, having designed a few residential homes and two shopping centres (Īģe and Spāre). He hadn't yet designed a library; this was his first.

But those in charge didn't like Armands' plan. It was too expensive, it wasn't very original either – educated architects should really have a more refined knowledge of these things without retreading old ground. These days, every shopping centre has an underground car park, and the commercial district is rife with parking spaces as well, both rented and for customers; what else were they going to defile the bowels of the Castle of Light with? Young Armands scoffed at the whole idea, and so he too turned on his heel and left for Ireland, to work as a cashier. After a couple of years, he dropped Katrīna a line saying he was happy there; he'd started a small architecture firm and said that if she was fed up with this place, she could go there; there'd always be work for her.

Maybe the commission was right, maybe Armands' design wasn't as good as he'd thought, but what could she say? Let him hone his skills in Ireland, it'll lead to good things for him in the end. Katrīna had already done her time abroad, in France. She had learned from that negative experience and left Paris to study in England. But to stay and live there? Brr! What was so bad about Latvia?

After her department colleague Leons left Latvia to work in a Volkswagen factory in Germany, Katrīna became the head of her department, her own boss, and was held accountable for systemising and overseeing the entire department – including all the books that had yet to be sent their way – new books from publishers, as well as donated ones, books that were really old and stuck together, pawed by greasy fingers, falling out of their covers. Katrīna knew them all, most of them, of course, by their number, but several by their covers. For example, 0810105907 belonged to the first department, so you had to put it on Cart 1. Likewise, 0521367370, with its brown cover and mustachioed man on it, belonged on Cart 1.2. A colleague would bring it to a reader, whoever had requested it. Not many people came here looking for information. A few, sure, but almost everyone had the internet at home by this point; they just came to search the library database, or read newspapers, or they'd just be dashing through to look something up in the encyclopaedia. No one had time for reading any more; they didn't let anyone take anything home, of course, it could only be used here, and the books were mostly rather thick and heavy, some weighed over half a kilo. There weren't too many visitors in the daytime, most people were at work or school; at night, a few pensioners would trickle in to flip through the newspapers. These low-income pensioners ended up here because of an urban integration project sponsored by the European Commission a few years back. Half of them were sent to direct traffic jams in Jugla, downtown, or in Piemārupe; the other half caught fare dodgers on trams, trolleybuses, and intercity buses. It made everyone feel useful; what more do old people need? They came in droves from the country seeking city fortunes. The Ministry of Agriculture sent out a press release claiming responsibility for those who commuted to the city. The country folk needed to relax, the press release said. You have to let the land lie fallow for a few years for the earth to recover. Later, they promised they'd devote their energy to developing a suitable environment for crops. For now, you just had to be patient, agriculture would be a national priority next year; this year, it was data processing and storage. The Year of the Castle of Light, you could say.

But that wasn't why country folk came looking for work in the city, or why they were overqualified to be traffic conductors and ticket collectors – they were already pinching every penny to supplement their pensions. No one had it easy in old age, and not just in Latvia – it was right there in that book (no number, Department 6R, copyright 1954) in black and white: 80 per cent of American residents didn't earn enough for their level of subsistence. Even though much had changed in America, there will always be people like those in the soap operas, and people who live in cardboard boxes on the street – 80 per cent. We had fewer lower income folk in Latvia, some 40 per cent, no more.

Katrīna's Grandma didn't consider herself one of the poor folk in Latvia and chose not to work – she was apparently fed up with working for 50 years; she wanted to see the world. She handed in her notice and went off to live with Mama in Ireland. That left Katrīna on her own in her massive three-room apartment in Pļavnieki, but at least she had her job, which she could reach directly now that the No. 18 had started running. On Sundays she could head off to the Old Town to walk around. Every now and then the antique houses set up a display in Dome Square: all sorts of wooden clogs, wood-carvings from the Arkādija Park movie theatre (beautiful, burned black, probably intentionally), faces, masks, dragons from renovated buildings in the city centre, and female nudes from former bank buildings. Katrīna walked along on her own looking at them, it didn't bring her the same joy it would have if her friend Elīze had been with her. They could have tittered about it to each other, but Elīze and Ilze were in England now. They didn't have a good relationship with Latvia. They had been looking for a place of their own for quite some time, found it, but couldn't get the apartment, since all the neighbours could tell why they wanted to live together – two women who weren't students and earned good money. They earned too little to have been able to save anything, but they were proud, impatient and as stubborn as goats. They wanted everything fast, they applied for a mortgage, but they didn't have good credit. So Ilze split on her advertising company and they were both off. Elīze knew they wouldn't earn as much as they did in Latvia, but they'd make up for it by being able to breathe. There's a lot to be said for breathing, but Katrīna no longer had anyone to talk to. At work, sure – smiling, calm, open, helpful colleagues. It was quiet there; when you felt like it, you could request music to sort books to. Sometimes Ms Anna, the cleaner, put on that fun song from the Ajax adverts, and the book sorting went twice as fast. Her colleagues travelled from the suburbs where there's no demand for books; those who still read, bought books for themselves and passed them on to others, so there weren't any visitors; you couldn't even hire an old lady to sit there for 100 lats, and anyway that money would be better spent on national development. And so, they built the Castle of Light – *raised over the black water,* cried the average woman and man, just like the old song – and everyone knew how tiny this country was; an old border river running through it, yet, right there in the middle of it, the legendary Castle of Light had materialised!

How many people in the world haven't been to see Katrīna's workplace, the face of the nation! The design competition was won by one of the younger architects; he didn't even have a degree, but he had an original and economical idea: he proposed building an artificial island between the Southern and Island Bridges (imagine that!) to serve as the foundations for the library. The Castle of Light was built so that it raised itself up over both bridges, every day reminding the people of the meaningless and finiteness of their insignificant existence from the past through the present and into the future – at least that's how it was explained in the ministry's development brochure, which according to tradition was encapsulated in the foundation of the island itself. No greenery; that wasn't really fashionable any more. No benches, but a fountain right across from the director's office; it was easier to draw the water straight there from the river. Everything was laid out in the clearest and most methodical way; rare books and archives at the very bottom. The walls meet under the water without letting the damp through, but the humidity feels almost as it would in a basement, with electric heaters to dry it out as needed.

They carefully selected those allowed to work here, rejecting former milkmaids, or anyone who claimed to have a liberal arts degree, which was of little use to anyone; they wrote jingles on their lunch break and read every book – good or bad – from cover to cover. They were looking for original, critically thinking people who knew how to choose the highest quality books, no chick lit or crime novels, no simple rhymesters; only classic and the most up-to-date writers and poets. The whole department, right up to the highest levels of the Ministry of Culture, evaluated every jobseeker, making them use the library system, retrieve things from the internet and different databases, identify barcodes. Then the Commission from the Ministry of Health subjected them to stressful situations; for example, they'd turn off the electricity to see what would happen – the person who turned on the generator and helped others get out of the building would become the subordinate, the one who ran away and saved themselves became the boss, and the one who ran around aimlessly didn't get hired. So clever! After a long debate among all the powerful organs of the Ministries of Health and Welfare, the Language Commission moved in and introduced new terms – broad intelligence and flexible thought. Broad intelligence was attributed to potential employees who took initiative on entry and exhibited an in-depth ability to think. Flexible thought, on the other hand, was associated with the ability to recognise the consequences of one's actions – this seemingly secondary trait of strength was actually valued highest. On the broad intelligence test, Katrīna had one of the highest scores, but she didn't do so well on the flexible thought test. A bit odd, since Katrīna was fairly certain of the consequences of her actions. But she passed the first part with flying colours. Whoever was left after that was interrogated with all sorts of questions in an attempt to provoke and confuse them; the goal was to make offers to open and intelligent employees. And they were wildly successful – not counting a few clowns, all the employees (89 per cent of them women) were precise, careful, considerate. Sometimes Katrīna filled in for her colleagues at lunch – incidentally, there was a cafeteria right there in the Castle of Light, economical in every aspect: it saved manpower resources, no one dawdling around the city shopping; it saved money on electricity that would be used if workers were let out one by one from the Castle of Light at lunch; it also earned a bit of money: the cafeteria paid the Ministry of Culture rent for the right to feed librarians and visitors.

One of the times Katrīna was filling in for a colleague, a visitor dashed in, a young mother wanting to show her son some cows, not digital illustrations, but the best photographs. And if they weren't available, then some old eighteenth- or nineteenth-century drawings from zoological texts. Katrīna rose to the challenge, even though helping readers wasn't at all part of her job description (she just sorted things by number). She searched the main catalogue, found it in Section 63, and showed them the damn cow! The kid was delighted, the mother even more so; she wanted to raise a veterinarian, since the little one had been interested in all sorts of animals from day one. *So she wants a mansion*, Katrīna thought, but bit her tongue, saying nothing in the end. What did it matter to her? Let them raise their kids however they want. Good thing the Ministry of Family Affairs was sensible enough to lift the ban on whipping kids for serious offences, otherwise they'd be rampaging through the streets like hooligans, not opening doors for women, yelling in shops, laughing in church, pressing the buttons at pedestrian crossings just for the hell of it. They should punish the parents! Let them clean the streets after work if they can't put a cork in Johnny or Peter's mouth at the sweet counter or during communion. Don't bring the snivellers to church if they can't sit for half an hour without snivelling. Hire a nanny to accompany them in public if you can't keep them in check and stop them from messing around with those damn buttons.

See, some school kids were getting on the tram again, but these were good ones; they sat still and looked out the window, they knew what animals behaved like. Now it was so simple – if they got too noisy, it was enough to wave angrily at the conductor – and they'd shut their mouths, and sit there like tiny mice under a raised broom, knowing that no one would think it a shame if they got smacked. And they would deserve it too. *Stop dancing like mice on the table,* she thought. *If only you knew what it was like in the old days!* But Katrīna never said anything out loud, she was smart enough not to; let them raise their kids however they want, it wasn't for her to interfere. You want to show them pictures of cows – go for it! You want to take them go-karting – take them then! Just as long as when your child doesn't grow up how you wanted, when he gets older and is grabbed by the horns and dragged off into the woods, you don't blame the kindergarten teachers, or the long queues everywhere, or a less than suitable psychological environment. You yourself are to blame! You didn't notice what you should have, you didn't hear what you should have, you raised him on the wrong TV shows and the wrong websites.

She would need to get off the tram soon. Out of habit, Katrīna checked to make sure she hadn't left her pass at home and got up. Next stop: National Library. She hoped no one would need their shift covering today; Katrīna didn't like having any contact with the readers. Katrīna had even written to Ivars in Australia about the cow incident (he was working there as a priest for a Latvian parish, you could always pour out your heart to him over email), and he suggested pulling up good old *Crocodile Dundee* on the internet; it had plenty of cattle and more besides. But Katrīna wasn't really into the exotic, what were spotted snakes and orange frogs to her? She grew uncomfortable thinking about how far away Ireland and Germany were, let alone Australia. What was strangest of all was how no one realised that you could stay right here, maybe even move up the ladder now that all those other folks were gone. The economy would grow (wages were paid by foreign businessmen, and were taxed according to the country where the worker came from – a new EU law. Those who stayed in Latvia got a tax break; if you weren't stupid – and Katrīna wasn't – you wouldn't pass that up), public transport would expand (with hardly any traffic jams, everyone would go about jovially, satisfied in their own contentedness), the job market would diversify (all sorts of new professions were being introduced by the Ministry of Welfare's Employment Service that year alone), new goods would get made (consumer goods and cultural goods, don't get too excited!), in short – the country would grow, and the Castle of Light was a perfectly justifiable talisman for such growth. Jeering and mocking didn't matter, cynics would get themselves worked up in vain – even in Europe they'd notice how Latvia was blossoming. How could you not be proud to live in such a progressive country? Katrīna looked on with pride as her workplace approached.

The Girl Who Cut My Hair

Kristīne Želve

Translated by Ieva Lešinska

I WAS SITTING IN a friend's flat: two large, almost empty rooms in a large, almost empty communal flat in the centre of the city. The mattress was on the floor; books were in piles on the floor; ashtrays were on the floor; untreated boards propped up on something or other posed as a desk; one wall had been roughly painted white to serve as a backdrop for portraits. We were having a serious talk. As usual, we were discussing what we could do together, and we were quite sure that we'd never do anything, at least not together. I found out recently that we're both typical melancholics (he has the characteristics of a phlegmatic melancholic; me, a choleric one), and the only thing that two melancholics can accomplish together is to agree that it makes no sense for them to do anything.

On seeing his belongings, and how similar they were to mine, (in the assessment of My Fine Friend: 'This doesn't look like the flat of a young lady at all, but rather that of some political refugees'), I thought about the fact that we were both 30 or, as they say, 30 plus or minus. We talked about his photography and he mentioned a girl who did make-up for his models. She is The Girl Who Cut My Hair, but I didn't know that then. I remembered this girl and remarked that I'd known her for a long time, a very long time, from the time when being 30 for me was associated only with the flat of a Young Lady, the flat of a Famous, Well-to-Do and Married Young Lady, and not with a mattress and books on the floor, never!

'She was in a mood, you know, some problems with her guy. He seems to have taken off or something,' my friend said casually, and I asked – without any real interest or desire for the information – who her guy was now – after all, I didn't know anything about her guys, just like she didn't know mine.

'The guy is called "Rabbit",' my friend said, and I shrieked in horror.

'Rabbit! Rabbit! Rabbit, you say? What woman at the age of thirty goes out with a guy whose nickname is RABBIT!' I shouted hysterically. Being 30, the mattress on the floor and now this, the man-Rabbit. It was too many fingers in the eye for a single day, and in a single eye – mine.

When I was growing up, I didn't know what to do with my youth. I wanted to *leave* it somewhere. So, for a long time, I left it alone.

At the time, I had no idea that – about ten years later, or, as they say, ten years plus or minus – I'd be living in a room where the spines of unread books would scream at me from all four corners. I was one of those girls who – possessing undefined, yet topographic-map-solid, inner convictions – roamed the streets, cafés and flats of Riga. At the time, the city was full of us, girls with whom, as Rilke wrote, life played games, spring after spring making them stretch out their arms for nothing until they go slack in the shoulders.

We wrote in our secret diaries, which, at the slightest opportunity, we would read aloud to anyone that would listen:

when the lost word has been lost, when the worn-out word has been worn out, when the lying word has lied, an unspoken word still remains. When the unfaithful people have become unfaithful, when the cold people have become cold and the remote ones remote, when the lying people have started to lie and the betraying ones to betray, there are still the unmet people.

Or:

I have no choice if I were a butterfly you would certainly be a rock if I became a rock you would be an Algerian wind if I were an Algerian wind you would be ancient like a coal iron oh no I will simply be a beast with red fur and tea-coloured eyes a rain-soaked beast that loves autumn more than night and fears thaws for it does not understand the sun but knows what it does a beast that lurks around and does not know how to sing or dance to crochet or to knit so look for me in a remote library where books do not resemble bricks but swaddled babies who cry in fear of their mother whose name is Jeanne and who wore her hair red before it was cut to the skin what remains you ask worry worry it will always find you comes a whisper from a pair of lips that you can't forget like the bride from the foreign village with a river running through that we called Semantics because you can always step into it and understand always understand the same thing only the same thing.

And so on, and so on ad nauseam.

We did our hair with sugar water, rouged our cheeks, put shadows on our eyelids with powdered crayons, and shortened our skirts ourselves.

We would wander into art exhibitions, stroll to and fro

among the frames and, as soon as somebody paid attention to us, we'd say: 'No, no, we can't, we're busy... Life awaits!', and then we would quickly make for the door.

We were virgins with condoms in our handbags.

Our parents had not read either Freud or Henry Miller, absolutely not.

We were always at the ready – what if life should suddenly start?

We had yet to find an answer to a single question, but we continued to ask them. Possibilities we judged to be more important than outcomes, and we planned everything we'd probably never do down to the last detail.

We were those girls Rilke was writing about, la la la!

That day – about, or, as they say, ten years ago, plus or minus – the day when I first met The Girl Who Cut My Hair, was Easter Sunday. My friend Simma was going to St John's Church that evening to partake of the body and blood of Christ along with the Easter sermon, or 'Easter vermin,' as her neighbour teased her. This neighbour was a legend. As a boy, he had met the poet Čaks; at least he claimed as much, and we had no reason not to believe him. That said, a little suspicion lingered on because this flat, in which we all found ourselves, was on a street named after Alexander Čaks, so perhaps it was the name of the street that provoked the old geezer to create a romantic falsification of his personal history... well, no big deal, let him. In any case, he was less tedious than the rest of the occasional old drunks who used to accost us in parks, railway canteens and on seaside dunes.

Anyway, I knew that I wasn't going to attend the 'Easter vermin' with her: I was yet to overcome the fear and anxiety caused by the 'Moment of Entering' and had no inkling back then of how important the realisation would be that 'Fear is Here to Stay'. The idea that I'd spend the rest of my life fighting and overcoming my fears hadn't yet driven me to despair, and the red wine seemed quite useful to the both of us. For me, to make me less afraid of the Moment of Entering, and for Simma – who is very tired of life – to fortify herself and, as she puts it, 'to gradually prepare to partake of the sacrament'.

Simma was telling me about a wonderful guy she'd met:

'I talked and he listened; he was really listening to me!' She just couldn't get over it. Iva was asleep in the next room, wearing white socks with soiled feet. She arrived the night before and had stood there in the stairwell, in her white socks, announcing that she'd run away from home – secretly – hence no shoes, just socks.

'Torturers, they are all torturers!' Iva wailed.

'They all' included her grandmother, whose hearing was not what it had been, so, in my opinion, it wouldn't have mattered if Iva had run away in studded boots; her mum, who often spent the night with A Man Who Had Suddenly Entered Her Life and thus might not have noticed Iva's disappearance for several nights. Simma and I exchanged weary we've-seen-it-all glances, poured Iva a glass of wine, and put her to bed.

'Last night I had a dream about the butterfly, the same butterfly that Ance dreamt about; a huge, spectacular butterfly, and I screamed for someone to save me and kill the butterfly,' Simma went on. We told each other about all of the dreams we'd had, and I got the feeling that it was as important as when I was a child and, from my bed, would stare at my curtains covered with red, running animals (a good choice for a nursery, but to me it looked like there was a forest fire and that was why the animals were running and red), and play at inventing new words.

In all these dreams the girls were in love and the men lonely.

'I dreamt that I was at Kārlis' place and there was this guy that I didn't know but was in love with. I slept next to him every other night; the rest I still spent with Kārlis. Me and the stranger slept next to each other, but nothing happened. His wife asked us what exactly was going on between us. "Nothing," we replied. "But you slept in the same bed," she said. "Ah, but it's natural," we countered. "It's Something Entirely Different." Then I bent down to put torn newspaper in the litter tray and my eyes met his. I gazed at him and smiled. I decided I'd choose him! I love him, I love him!'

'I dreamt that I was in a room where, opposite the beds, there were toilets with hooks on their doors. I locked myself in one of the toilets with a guy called Andris Leimanis, I stroked his hair and back. He sat on my lap. He talked about his music again. We went outside, and I ate. There were peas and mushrooms to eat.'

'In my dream, he was with me again; we were lying on a low bed and directly above us there was an open window and the fresh spring air made the light green curtain flap. The curtain was thin like a newly opened, still sticky leaf. "Why don't you take your clothes off?" I asked him. "I can't," he said. "I would feel like a shipwreck."'

The doorbell rang; it was Dainuvīte. She'd come over to pick up Simma to go to the Easter vermin and partake of the body and the blood of Christ.

On seeing Simma, Dainuvīte started yelling: 'But look at you. You are drunk, you're pissed! You can't go to church and accept the holy sacrament in that state!'

'I already accepted the sacrament!' Simma shot back.

'Don't you blaspheme! How could you accept the holy sacrament in your house!?;

'But, Dainuvīte,' Simma pronounced these two words in a deliberate and authoritative fashion. Adding a measure of reproach, she repeated with emphasis: 'But, Dainuvīte,

CHRIST never said that the holy sacrament could only be received in church. It's an invention of false prophets! CHRIST HIMSELF has NEVER said that! There is nothing about it in the Bible! Nothing! I don't have to go to church to receive the sacrament, I can do it anywhere, any time... That's what the Bible says, the Bible says: "...and turn to me wherever you are..." That's what CHRIST HIMSELF said! Go ahead, Dainuvīte, read it!'

Dainuvīte nodded, and Simma simmered down. 'We are all horizontal in the eyes of God. On the same level, the line of the horizon. Like waves in the sea!' she managed to add.

Although the sacrament had been received outside the church, they went to listen to the Easter sermon. I accompanied them and so did the tortured white-socked, black-footed Iva who had borrowed Simma's shoes.

Springtime always made me feel like eating black, damp earth. To grab it by the handful and bring it up to my face! Cutting through a square in the Old Town, our foursome ran into two other girls; one of them would become The Girl Who Cut My Hair, but the two of us didn't know that yet. That would happen ten years later or, ten years plus or minus, as they say.

We were standing there, a gaggle of girls in the ever so slowly blue-blackening spring twilight swapping stories. A man walked past, he asked us for the time. Oh no, he wasn't attempting a Pick-Up Conversation, he was only interested in the time. We had no watches, I was pretty sure of it, yet The Girl Who Cut My Hair said: 'One moment!' and slid her hand into the pocket of her overcoat. A smooth, softly shimmering light-blue atlas ribbon appeared from the pocket of The Girl Who Cut My Hair; one of those ribbons they used to tie around a swaddled baby to signal: *it's a boy!*

('How many hopes/ how much joy/ are in these words/ oh, it's a boy!' would read the inscription on a card from the

U.S. I would receive one day on the birth of my son. What Americans write if it's a girl who happens to be born, I haven't had a chance to find out).

The Girl Who Cut My Hair let the ribbon slither out of her pocket, centimetre by centimetre, metre by metre... All of us, even the random man, were mesmerised by the blue ribbon. We were incredulous, awaiting a miracle. The Girl Who Cut My Hair was a magician producing a blue ribbon from a top hat, and at the end of the ribbon, there was

a rabbit!

no!

a dove!

no!

a watch tied with a huge knot!

yes!

And instead of a heavy, aristocratic, brass pocket watch from the interwar period, it was the most banal kind: a Soviet-produced man's wristwatch – a Zarya or something – tied to the end of a light blue atlas ribbon.

'Ten to ten,' The Girl Who Cut My Hair announced solemnly.

It was a string of words understood solely by the denizens of planet Earth. That was the next philosophical theme we discussed that evening, perched on the back-rests of park benches in the Old Town square, until the spring sky turned black and we scattered to our parents' flats.

I did not see her again for the next ten years – or ten years plus or minus – but then, one day, I went to a good hairdressing salon and she cut my hair.

As a child, I had dreamt of having a braid. I couldn't quite recall why my parents decided to let my sister grow her hair out but cut mine. In all likelihood, it wasn't really a decision, just one of those things. In my imagination, I had always seen myself with a long, blonde braid, just like the one my classmate Lolita Vilciṇa had. I could feel it hanging down past my shoulders; how individual hairs had freed themselves from the braid and stuck to my white jumper. I imagined that, when I ran, the braid would bounce against my right shoulder, then against the left one, back and forth like the rope of a church bell. But, alas, so much for my dream braid. Several times I tried to grow my hair out but ended up cutting it.

The first time it was out of sheer foolishness. That year, all the girls cut their hair; and bleached it in front and poured sugar water on the ends, backcombing it before going to the discotheque. Me too.

'Look at the do on me and my friend here. We look like a pair of monkeys!' said my friend Sarmīte, showing me a photo from her secondary school days. I have the same photos in my own album: my friend and I at my sister's graduation, among mums and grans, done up like a pair of monkeys.

The second time, I cut my hair really, really short, barely a centimetre long; a real crew cut.

'Brave girl,' muttered the hairdresser, who had long hair with highlights, and just kept cutting. Back then, I wasn't quite the same kind of fool, I wanted a change in my life or something. That's what they all claim in women's magazines, don't they? Just cut your hair and a new life sets in, snip-snip-snip. Did I get a new life? Nuh-uh, the old one continued for a little while longer and only then did it occur to me that maybe the life I was longing for was my old life, the way it was before... But it was too late. The hair was cut off, the new life was snip-snip-snip upon me and I started to grow out my hair again.

It took years for me to grow my hair out, and it was bloody hard work too. My hair was fine and brittle, but I was determined to grow it – long, beautiful blonde hair.

Once a month, at waxing moon, I trimmed the ends: one centimetre per month.

Shampoo & conditioner.

Nourishing hair mask.

Hair oil treatment.

Shampoo for volume, mousse for volume.

The round hairbrush.

Vitamins in ampoules.

Revitalizing elixir.

Growth capsules.

Oil for the ends, lotion for the roots.

Shine treatment.

Hairdryer, speed 1, long prongs, circling motion and finally, hairspray.

For years I had spent two hours every day on my hair; my long, beautiful hair. Two hours a day. Seven hundred twenty-four hours per year. Two thousand one hundred seventy-two hours in three years. Amen.

Until one day I came across a good salon and saw her there: the girl I had not seen for ten years or, as they say, for ten years plus or minus.

On that day, she turned from The Girl with a Watch on a Blue Ribbon into The Girl Who Cut My Hair.

My well-groomed hair, grown with such tremendous effort.

Two thousand one hundred seventy-two hours.

2172 hours!

A White Jacket with Gold Buttons

Vilis Lācītis

Translated by Uldis Balodis

VALDIS SPALVUMS HAD POSITIONED himself as a refined Latvian man of letters, free of any unwanted cultural influences. He considered his use of the www.draugiem.lv[1] social network his patriotic duty and for several years his profile picture had remained the same, depicting him in a black T-shirt brandishing the slogan *NO, I'M NOT ON F!#$%ING FACEBOOK!!!* Though he was 40, Spalvums lived alone and was single, which he explained with the unadulterated bluntness of a poet: as a perfectionist, he could only accept a woman who never broke wind. No one like that could exist, so Spalvums' life came to be somewhat reclusive, tending towards the meditative.

He lived simply in a stylishly decorated apartment in Āgenskalns with central heating and a still functioning wood-burning stove. A few retro pieces of furniture and a Mac on his desk – that was enough for him. Just like its owner, everything in the apartment was clean, tidy, and orderly. The colour scheme was dominated by greys and greens with a sepia-toned poster from the hipster market hung on the pristine white bathroom door.

Spalvums' inner creative fire burned up the body fat, which plagued so many other middle-aged men and kept his figure lean and athletic. His thin legs and slight feet were tightly hugged by stylish jeans and sneakers. When on foot, he would zip across the Stone Bridge and, although some passers-by would flash him a crooked smirk, Spalvums knew how to ignore people like that, giving instead his attention to the Pārdaugava sky.

He sent his work off to every contest, however few there were in the limited Latvian literary milieu. He wrote his blog (spalvums.wordpress.com) and read and critiqued others' publications. As a critic, Spalvums would hold authors to the strictest possible standards. Until now the author who had received the highest praise from him was the epiphanist Sadegsnis for his posthumous volume, *The Pain within Me*:

> A splendid work. It seems almost like there's nothing to complain about, and yet something unsettles me. The misfortune lies in the fact that I like it. It's really good!
>
> I read it again.
>
> What could be bad about it?
>
> What's bad about it is that it's not genius. From a literary work I expect 'hyperquality,' I missed that which followed through to make it a world class hit. I expect an author to use the brilliance of his intellect to knock me off my feet and smear me across the walls. I have to admit that just for a moment the late author started to do just that, but ultimately failed. Our simpletons and good guys here are just too weak to smear Spalvums across anything.

In other words, Spalvums was an unwavering aesthete with a deep understanding of prose and poetry – and as such, he held himself in high regard. Now and again he would publish a poetry or prose collection, though usually those did not do so well.

'Readers can't take the truth and so they're too afraid to buy it,' Spalvums said commenting on the low number of copies he'd sold and continued working. His most recent published work was a collection of stories entitled *People with Broken Legs*. As the name suggests, this collection was devoted to small business owners in Latvia, inspired primarily by financial news and the paintings of Vilhelms Purvītis.

One sunny morning Spalvums made some coffee, sprinkled in some sugar and a little bit of cinnamon, opened up his laptop, and typed his name into Google. *People* had already been on the store shelves long enough for someone to finally have something to say about it.

And, indeed, on the poetry website Dzejdari.lv there was a recent review. But glancing at the author's name, Spalvums' brow furrowed. Arnolds Pabrēka was a no less prominent literary figure than Spalvums himself. It was Pabrēka who regularly organised *Readings from Poets Who Died This Month* at the Magone Culture Centre. He had also arranged for the European Union funding necessary for the publication of the calendar entitled *Let's Remember*. Each month's page featured a photo of a particular poet's gravestone with an appropriate accompanying text. For example, *December: a month of darkness and cold in which Eduards Veidenbaums falls ill with tuberculosis.*

In the 90s, Pabrēka had published the poetry collection *A Sonnet for a Cow*. These lines, which were revolutionary at that time, flowed from his pen:

A Cow loped across the meadow shiddin' itself,
It was hassled by a Gadfly and attacked by a Mosquito.

Pabrēka considered himself to be the creator of the style of 'rustic realism' (not to be confused with Russian or racist), because he had managed to convince the publisher to use the spelling 'shiddin' with a 'd and n, because that's how they talk where I'm from', as well as writing the names of every living creature with a capital letter, thereby showing respect for nature. Since 1993, Pabrēka had tirelessly asserted that all later works written in this way are to be classified as written in the rustic style.

Unfortunately, *Sonnet* didn't receive even a scrap of the recognition Spalvums' first collection *Cowdrop: Rural Realities.* received from its narrow readership. Following its publication, the term 'rural realism' (not to be confused with the rustic kind!) became entrenched in the jargon of a selection of literary critics. There weren't many of them, it's true, but there were even fewer who knew of *Sonnet*. As a result, Pabrēka had grown bitter. He complained that with Spalvums' undermining term 'rural realism', he was just sowing confusion in the already complicated Latvian literary environment. Pabrēka would go out and buy each and every one of Spalvums' poetry and prose collections, so he could publish ruinous critiques of them later on.

That guaranteed at least some sales for the books, but did Spalvums deserve this kind of scorn for that reason?

And now Pabrēka had completely inappropriately chosen to compare *People* with the first poetry collection of that dilettante and novice Azrāns! Spalvums sipped his cinnamon latte and began to read.

This time I'll write about two of our own homegrown authors: one of them has already long graced us with his work, but the other only recently took that risk for the first time. I'm talking of course about the recently published books by Valdis Spalvums and Teodors Heinrihs Azrāns.

Through his prose, Spalvums attempts to demonstrate that he knows suffering. Regrettably, one can only conclude that he does not really succeed.

Reading the collection *People with Broken Legs*, descriptions of depression and mental illness from other Latvian works come involuntarily to mind and the comparison with these, it must be said, does not do Spalvums any favours. And so, nothing else remains but to point out to the distinguished author that in truth the misery he feels is fairly banal and could be easily overcome with some kind of stipend from the European Union.

On the other hand, a truly excellent example of Weltschmertz, as authentic as a nerve laid bare by tooth decay, is Azrāns' first poetry collection *Creatures Crushed by my Fingernail*. The text is interwoven with authentic pain, undeniable misery, and true harshness. Azrāns does not just agonise according to our best national traditions. No, with his depressive sensory palette and the directness of his monologue, he pours out his personal bitterness. Harsh? Yes, but how captivating and refreshing is this kind of heartfelt coldness! Each line of every poem drives itself deeper into one's soul − like a fence post driven into earth blighted by frost. Rephrasing the book's title poem, 'Oh! yearning to shout, oh, but stop and give it a rest, I beg of you, I collapse and ask again and still more − oh, settle down, cruel poet!'

But the beauty of poetry can also be somewhat... cruel. Misery, which transcends the comprehensive abilities of the mind, literally flows out across each page as if the chambers of one's own heart were being drained, and soaks each line with rheumatic sensations. In this also lies Azrāns' talent: from the first pain-filled twinge, it's impossible to stop or to pull away.

To ache beyond measure. To feel stung with no end. To breathe transcendence... And so it goes, all the way through, each line, following every punctuation mark.

With such a powerful debut to compare it with, *People*, even with broken legs, still only limps along and does not create a sufficiently convincing image of malaise and difficulty.

Spalvums knew that Pabrēka's shrieking was nothing other than the product of his green-eyed envy. He stood up and looked down contemptuously at the words on the screen, then sat back down again. Seething on the inside, he clicked on 'Add a Comment'. In the 'Author' field he entered 'A Latvian man of letters'. In the 'Text' field, he wrote the following:

Listen, do you hear? A clock is marking time in this silence. I'm sitting alone in the big city and the grey walls of this building are telling me all about everything that's absent from my room: about liveliness and splendour, about beauty and greatness. Like the glittering play of colours at the circus, for example. I close my eyes and the ticking transforms into circus drums and trumpets.

Everyone calling themselves 'a creative' has gathered here in this tent. Look, the front row is filled with leeches attached to state cultural funding, still moist from having just wriggled out of the money pond. Look, right behind their slimy backs are the Euro-sponges. And all around there's a collection of different cloth daubers and theatre masks scattered across the seats, each fanning themselves with brochures and flyers for their own work.

I love all of them, every single one of them in this tent. Thin girls in spangle-covered skirts are swivelling their hips as they march along the edge of the arena. The girls all flash a flattering grin and the eyes of the old lechers light up. The band unleashes a tango and the creatives begin to happily sway along.

I'm standing in the back and breathe in deeply the presence of sawdust and elephants. I watch the orgy from the side through a gap in the curtains. I'm ready, I'm wearing a snow-white suit. I fix my tie. I quickly run my fingers over my perfectly polished row of buttons. I check if my lighter works. I quickly touch the umbrella I've hung off my belt. I wait until the tango ends, then raise and quickly lower my arm giving my assistants the signal.

In a flash the girls are gone from the arena, in their place my assistants roll out a large, old-fashioned cannon to the very centre, tilting its huge, fat barrel upwards. Darkness covers the tent; the band starts playing an anxious tune. Its melody moves out across the assembled crowd as it falls silent.

'Click' goes my Zippo. Its flame touches the soaking wet torch and it is instantly covered with blue and yellow flaming flowers. I step out into the arena and stand in the centre holding the torch high with my left hand. The crowd is frozen in anticipation. The band fluidly increases its tempo and switches to a march. The barrel is pointing directly at the tent's zenith. Darkness surrounds me, but I don't even need to tax my imagination to see every one of those well-known faces and envision their idiotically twisted expressions.

I pull out my umbrella and press the button on the handle. The march the band is playing reaches an almost deafening volume. I'm now protected by a large, black dome made of extremely durable fabric. The march speeds up to a hysterical pace, it's amazing that the drummers are able to move their hands so quickly.

Without further ado, the torch moves downward and a blinding explosion blasts across the arena, consuming all other sound in its wake. For just a moment the white smoke from the gunpowder is illuminated by the light of the explosion. A dark cloud shoots up into the air and then, beholden to gravity, rains across the earth. The umbrella in my hand shakes convulsively from the impacts.

Finally, the last few strikes. The rain stops. With a careless motion I toss away the umbrella, which falls down a few metres away from me.

In the next moment, floodlights turn on all around the arena. The tent is brightly illuminated. Every single row of spectators is covered with shit.

And I'm standing right in the centre of it all, in a white jacket with gold buttons.

One little detail that nobodies like Pabrēka will never manage to understand is the true nature of art. Real art can happen only when you forget about the haters and the wilfully ignorant and fearlessly turn your soul inside out in front of everybody. Writing is, in a sense, close to psychoanalysis: the power of the written word comes exactly from the fact that an author spits out his most hidden feelings, without the shiny veneer that comes from pretending.

And now at last Spalvums felt a sense of accomplishment, this time for real. With a feeling of a job well done, he clicked 'Add Comment' and went to make himself another cup of coffee.

Notes

1. Draugiem.lv (draugiem meaning 'for friends') is a Latvian social network, which until recently outcompeted Facebook in Latvia.

Where I Am

Andra Neiburga

Translated by Uldis Balodis

SPRING HAS JUST BEGUN to fill the trees and parks with a splash of green. Not only have snowdrops already pushed through the earth next to the cathedral in the Esplanade, but there are some crocuses too. Even the barbed-wire fences surrounding the park are starting to look almost spring-like; it seems as if, at any moment, they might also sprout flowers. But the mud on the potholed streets has not yet dried and, as the snow melts, it reveals all kinds of rubbish that has collected during the winter. The city is waiting for the return of the street cleaner.

All along one side of Brīvības Street – just a short distance from the Esplanade and the Nativity Cathedral – stands an old two-story wooden home, recently purchased by the flax producer Bertrams. The family's apartments occupy the entire second floor. Ten rooms in enfilades; a dark corridor, the ceiling covered with frescoes, oak panels. The Bertrams know that the day will eventually come when this building will be torn down and a modern stone building constructed in its place.

Gaisma,[1] the Bertrams family cow, can also sense the approach of spring. From the barn in their courtyard, she moos emphatically each morning until Hele, their maid, takes her out and walks her down to Bilderliņi, the part of town where the wealthy gentlemen have their summerhouses. There she grazes on the grass that has been planted under the apple trees. Grazing is not a simple business in Jūrmala. For growing children, it is said that there's nothing better than whole, full-fat milk. During the summer, the Bertrams' cow would give as much as 11 quarts every day, which meant that there was always some leftover to sell to the neighbours.

But for now, Gaisma has to be patient, and so do her owners. Winters in Riga are so long and dark that they seem to be almost endless.

Elma Bertrams dislikes going to ladies' afternoons and even less to charity balls. But she has no say in the matter; she must force herself to go, because that is what's demanded by good manners – and by her husband, Ansis Bertrams. She is expected to put on the heavy Egyptian-style, emerald necklace that Ansis gave her, and then go and show everyone how rich and powerful the Bertrams family are. Whenever she has a moment to spare, Elma paints watercolours. Flowers are her favourite. Elma enjoys painting nature scenes. However, in winter it's difficult to find flowers in Riga. All winter long, she yearns for fields and flowers. When the summer arrives, Elma paints nasturtiums, poppies, pansies, and all manner of meadow flowers, whatever is in front of her: marsh marigolds and globeflowers, corn flowers and daisies. Still, there isn't much free time. And even though they have a maid for the house and an English governess for the children, Elma still has to go to the market, has to manage the kitchen herself, and there is always something to be patched or mended.

Recently, the same as every spring, there has also been a seamstress at the house.

The seamstress only finished her work last Wednesday, Elma writes in a letter to her sister Zuze.

I've already grown completely bored with it all. I didn't have anything sewn for me. I didn't feel like buying new cloth, and couldn't come up with any fresh new style that would work for any of my old things. Besides, I can always wear my folk costume to official functions; I just need to mend the lace along the edge of the skirt. By the way, did you hear that Elza's cow ate nails and wire and so had to be slaughtered? Elza had written right away that Kristīne should sell the meat, but there hadn't been any takers. So, today Elza went with Bērziņš to Robeži, bringing the meat, as well as the hide, along with them. Tomorrow we'll have to go sell it somewhere.

Elma writes to her sisters Elza, Zuze, and Kate nearly every day, and they to her. This has been their habit since their years as refugees in Russia, though the mail was often delayed back then so their letters would tend to arrive three or four at a time. But worst of all was the mail service during the Stučka[2] years – Elza's husband, a minister, was murdered by Stučka's henchmen. They stabbed him with their bayonets in eighteen different places; news of which only arrived in Riga three weeks later.

Not so long ago, Elma would write to her sisters in German, other times in Russian, but now she has her own country with its own language. In the beginning, it was not that easy for her to switch to writing in Latvian. Her handwriting is even and clear, her sentences smooth and rounded. Elma and her sisters – all four of them daughters of a rural schoolteacher – had received a good education. Much better than her husband Ansis who had spent his childhood herding farm animals and had, at most, sat for three years at a school desk. But who would be able to notice that nowadays?

I spent the whole of last week mending things. The sheets had gotten pretty worn through this winter, the towels too. Mother's old towels were like a sieve in places, but they remind me of being young and so I just don't want to throw them out. I've bought a few new ones and I'll monogram them myself. Zuze sewed me a beautiful yellow tablecloth with baskets of blue cornflowers for my birthday. I'll take that with me to Bulduri. When Jāzeps comes to Riga again, have him bring me a cutting or two from that black gooseberry bush, I'll put it here in our yard, then later I'll plant it in Bilderliņi. Mother is crazy about those gooseberries.

*

'Mother, what's flirting?'

Jānis is studying a magazine. *Love and Flirting* is written across its cover. At least love is quite clear, but what about flirting?

'Flirting?' Elma jumps up. '*Lass das!*'[3] she yells more harshly than she would have liked.

It's shameful that a magazine like that is even in their home. Such a lewd rag. Elma would never have allowed it, but Uncle Arvēds – his mind growing feeble in his old age – bought it from Tupiņš, the tabloid publisher. Ansis had brought the magazine home to have a look at it. If only that devil Tupiņš would go bust. You have to be careful not to end up in the pages of a magazine like that (though some people actually long for it, it seems.) As far as Uncle Arvēds is concerned, Elma would rather just not see him anymore. All kinds of filth, all kinds of Piccadillies, Trocaderos, Foxtrott-Dieles,[4] and Arvēds was always right there, with his insatiable appetite for wine and food and his anecdotes and tales of the opera corps de ballet. There are even gentlemen's evenings at some of those night clubs where barmaids dance showing their bare breasts, and where members of parliament and government ministers have been spotted. Where will the country end up, travelling along a path like this one? Writing in the *Jaunākās Ziņas*,[5] in what most likely amounts to an exercise in complete futility, the Latvian authors Viktors Eglītis and Anna Brigadere harshly criticised these gossip rags, accusing them of being a corrupting influence on the Latvian nation. All of this nonsense has been brought here from the West, they argue, and now Riga wants to be just as fancy as a big city like Paris.

Elma knows what Paris is like. Earlier this year she and Ansis had been on a grand European tour. They visited Paris, Cannes, Nice, Capri, Monte Carlo, and Saint-Rémy.

All of it was beautiful, but somehow foreign. Elma didn't really enjoy herself. In truth, she can only really relax and enjoy herself in the countryside. And though these foreign lands were colourful and often breathtaking, Latvia was somehow more dear.

> We wanted to buy more things for ourselves in Paris, but among all the manufactured goods there's so much Schund[6] that it makes you not even want to look at any of it, and anyway, well-made items are expensive even here, in Riga. In the boutiques and stores of Paris, with nice things on display, sometimes no prices are given, and I find the experience, as a foreigner, quite unpleasant. And when prices are shown, like in the big Kaufhauses, then the problem is that the quality of those goods is very poor. Ansis bought himself a coat made of English cloth and paid 650 Fr., and I only bought myself one Crepe de Chine dress with a little bit of gold stitching and paid 275 Fr. Fancier dresses cost 500-600 Fr.

She and Ansis did not visit a single night club or café-chantant, just museums and theatres, the only exception being a brief game of chance in Monte Carlo. Absolutely everyone there was dressed even fancier than at the opera, and behaved very respectably.

Elma is mending the flesh-coloured stockings she brought from Paris. Although not very durable, these are the types of stockings the women over there are wearing these days; only the occasional old dear can be seen on the street in black stockings. In rainy weather, the Parisian ladies walk around in short skirts, their shins speckled with mud. Whereas in Riga, the majority of women still wear longer skirts, the hems of which are stained black from sloshing through the muddy city streets. The Bertrams family owns one of the first automobiles in Riga, a genuine Rolls-Royce. It sits in their garage out in the yard between the Bertrams' barn and their coachman Ivanovs' stables. Ansis drives the car to his factories, but the family only get to drive around on special occasions, or long journeys, such as when they go to Bilderliņi or Robeži.

'Put that magazine down,' Elma says, but this time not as harshly.

The boy gets poked, sharply as if with a needle, right in the spot where his forehead, eyebrows and nose meet; so sharply that his eyes fill with tears. For some reason, it seems like this has more to do with the name and appearance of the magazine than with his mother's rebuke. He quickly pushes the magazine away from himself. The picture on the cover shows a lady with a heavy bosom and a man in a suit with a round face and stomach, and a strange grin. There is a cigarette in a long holder in the woman's hand and a delicate twist of smoke is rising from it, winding almost like a noose around the man's neck. The man looks a bit like his father Ansis, but it isn't him.

His mother Elma said recently at lunch that, in Monte Carlo, even the older ladies go to dinner in sleeveless dresses with their cleavage on show, seemingly unashamed of their old, flabby arms. Latvians still have much to learn about how to behave and how to dress. In Cannes, Elma and Ansis had ended up in a hotel that was a little too fancy; it was almost exclusively English society there. The first evening, Ansis had gone down to dinner dressed in his dark suit coat, but every other man was wearing a smoking jacket and the ladies were in their evening dresses. There was nothing to do but get out the smoking jacket the next night.

Jānis thinks his parents' stories are interesting, but his sister Sofija only crinkles her nose and, when their parents are out of earshot, mutters about their ignorance and lack of sophistication.

Their maid, Hele, appears at the door:

'Uh… do you really want intestine soup today?'

'Yes, just like I said!'

Intestine soup is Ansis' favourite food but Hele doesn't like preparing it; so much work for something so disgusting. Although the intestines from the butcher shop have already been cleaned, there is still a considerable amount of rinsing involved and Hele becomes nauseous just glancing at those pale coils.

Hele is half-Estonian, from just near the border, and before joining the Bertrams family, she had worked in Reval.[7] No one there asked her to make intestine soup. Her employers were more refined. In Hele's opinion, everything in Estonia is, for the most part, better – the streets are cleaner and less potholed, and they have more Chinese lanterns on their Independence Day. These are some of the reasons, Hele feels, why she is better than the other servants, and perhaps more cultured than her employers. On free evenings, Hele goes to the cinema. There are more than 30 movie theatres in Riga, so in that respect at least it is far ahead of Reval; Hele has to acknowledge and accept that. The recently opened Splendid Palace, the finest

movie theatre in Riga, is located right around the corner from
the Bertrams. All of the movie premieres take place there, but a
ticket costs 2 lats so only wealthy gentlemen can afford to go,
smartly dressed to match their magnificent surroundings. Each
screening is accompanied by a first-rate live orchestra. Hele goes
to the cinema on Marijas Street, or sometimes travels to
Griškene, where tickets cost only 5 santīms (though the film
stock is pretty worn out there). She spends much of what she
makes on seeing movies, and at night passes endless hours using
coloured pencils to trace over actors' portraits on playbills she
secretly takes or on postcards she buys at the kiosk. Like
everybody, Hele likes movies about Tarzan's adventures, and has
traced many portraits of Elmo Lincoln. She thinks that Elmo
might actually be an Estonian.

After spending half the night drawing, morning comes
and Hele is tired and irritable. She sends her drawings to her
mother in Valka, adding a few short notes about current events
in Riga on the back. Following the division of Valka between
Estonia and Latvia in 1920, Hele's mother ended up on the
Latvian side, but all of the most important cultural and
financial institutions in the city stayed on the Estonian side –
in Valga. Of course, they did.

Hele, muttering something to herself in Estonian, walks
back in the direction of the kitchen, and Elma leans over her
letter again.

*You'll probably want to know something about Paris
fashions. It seems brown is the most popular colour, especially
lighter tones from sand to rust. You also see many red dresses,
often with black. Reddish purple is something new, it looks
almost like a fuchsia blossom. On the streets you mostly see
smaller hats being worn, though larger ones are already
starting to appear in shop windows. The tips of shoes are
becoming wider and only evening shoes still have slightly*

narrower ones. We caught up with Natālija and Olga in Nice. They had wanted to help me pick out a coat, but nothing came of it, because coats are worn shorter than dresses and I didn't like that at all. But at least we learned that Mr Lazdiņš and his daughter are in San Remi and that it's much less expensive there than in France, so we went there soon afterwards.

Jānis cautiously drags the magazine back toward himself and slides it underneath his coat.

'Should I go, then?'

'Go and see if you can help Hele with anything.'

The boy leaves the room.

When he looks closer, the image on the cover does really look like his father. But it's not his father, surely.

The boy doesn't turn to go towards the kitchen as instructed, but instead knocks on his sister Sofija's door.

'*Ein Moment, bitte!*'[8]

Sofija opens the door and Jānis can smell the cigarette smoke immediately.

His sister is sixteen and is studying at the French lycée. Almost all the girls in her class secretly smoke. Well, maybe not all of them, and not every day, but still. And yet, not all of them are allowed to cut off their braids and wear their hair short. Sofija was only allowed to do so after long discussions with her family. Maybe it was thanks to her parents' trip across Europe. There they had been able to experience life in a more open-minded society, at least that's what Sofija thought. Now her short, black hair squarely frames her narrow face with its expressive, black eyebrows. Jānis is completely blonde and everyone is amazed by Sofija's pale skin and black hair. She likes the way she looks, because the most beautiful and smartest girl in her class, Marī, has the same hairstyle. Marī is the daughter of a very wealthy businessman. Her mother never has to mend anything of her own, and she doesn't need to go to the market with the maid – she sleeps in and wears a long string of pearls around her neck every day, even at home. They have many books, many more than in Ansis' library, as well as numerous paintings, which are nothing like those hanging on the walls of the Bertrams family home. That's cubism, Marī told her once, pointing at a small drawing by the famous French artist Picasso.

Sofija also wants to be like that. She is already beautiful and works hard at school so that, later, she might even be able to study abroad. Sofija knows that many Latvian artists, like Strunke, Grosvalds, and Suta, went to Europe, mainly Paris, to find inspiration for their own art. She could experience real life there. She could become a Bohemian. When her friends return from their various sojourns, they look like real Parisians, not like her parents Elma and Ansis. Sofija reads Breton, Éluard, and Aragon as Marī regularly receives books sent by her relatives in France.

'You're a genuine intellectual,' says Jānis gently mocking Sofija as he waves away a cloud of cigarette smoke. 'And how's it even possible that Mother hasn't found out about your smoking yet?'

Sofija speaks five languages fluently: Latvian, Russian, German, French, and English. In school she is studying Latin and is also teaching herself Estonian, even though she doesn't have any great interest in the Estonians or their language. Just like Latvians, they are a people bound up and numbed by northern darkness. Some of the girls in her class are as obsessed with Buddhism as she is with French literature. Karl Tõnisson[9] is their idol with his bald head, crazy eyes, and his horrible, long beard that splits in two. In Sofija's opinion he is a cheat and a charlatan. He opened a Buddhist temple in Riga at 8 Baložu Street and a few of Sofija's classmates – those most spellbound by him – had secretly gone there for prayers. Sofija is only vaguely interested in all of that, but remembered that Hele is Estonian, and felt that a spare language wouldn't hurt. In exchange for help with her pronunciation, Sofija sometimes pays for her movie ticket. This also helps keep Hele from telling anyone about her smoking.

Jānis has no luck with languages. He can at least speak a bit of German. Russian not at all; he hadn't spent half his childhood living as a refugee in Russia like his sister had. In Latvia, the children had an English governess, but Jānis never spoke with her at all. What was there to talk about?

'Were you smoking?'

'Yeah.'

'Give me one too!'

'Idiot.'

'Look what I've got!' Jānis pulls the magazine out from under his arm.

'What's that?'

'It's Uncle Arvēds' new magazine.'

Sofija snatches the magazine out of her brother's hands, thumbs through it, reads a little bit here and there, and snorts dismissively: 'Shit.'

She says 'shit' with the greatest of pleasure. Saying it was completely forbidden both in their family home and at school.

'That's not literature, that's just shit.'

She carelessly throws the magazine on the floor, pulls out a silver case from underneath her pillow, and draws out two cigarettes, long and dark. She lights both and hands one to her brother.

'Well? Take it.'

'Uh…' Jānis is dumbfounded. He didn't mean it seriously. But now he has no choice but to smoke it. He takes a drag; it feels pretty good. It doesn't even make him cough. He takes another puff.

ANDRA NEIBURGA

'A magazine like this one demeans women,' Sofija declares. 'In France, all educated women are free, not slaves to their husbands and boyfriends! Women can visit bars and cabarets – as customers, not just as barmaids! And just in general, society there isn't so limited in its understanding of human rights.'

Jānis shakes his head, partly in disapproval, partly in disbelief, and feels a hint of light-headedness coming over him, along with a feeling of nausea.

'And a woman has rights in her sexual life. Even a woman and a woman, or a man and a man, can live together. Things like that don't upset anybody there.'

Oh Lord, what's she even talking about, Jānis thinks to himself and sinks back into the pillows as the ceiling starts to spin.

'And did you hear – yesterday at the Guild Hall in the Old Town here in Riga they had the "Modern Woman's Court" again and the hall was positively overflowing! Listen to what Eglītis wrote…'

Sofija grabs the newspaper and starts to read:

Our women are divided into three large groups: women labourers, women working in intellectual jobs, and women who don't work. I won't discuss the woman labourer in any more detail. Her life is her work. A person who is yoked and shackled has no time for debauchery.

'Ha, ha, women, beasts of burden, as if slave-work guaranteed innocence and chastity!'

The woman working an intellectual job moves between being like the woman labourer and the woman who doesn't work. The difficulties she has in her life connect her to the woman labourer, but her psychology and mindset make her more like the woman who doesn't work.

'Did you hear? An intelligent woman is ruined just because she has time to think! But you know, when I grow up, I'm leaving. I'll study at the Sorbonne. They take women as students there, too. Marī is also going to study there. Philosophy. Or maybe I'll become an artist.'

Jānis has fallen asleep. Sofija kisses her brother on his cheek and takes the smoking cigarette from his hand as its long column of ashes drops on to the floor.

The spring light shines softly through the winter-tarnished window panes. Jānis is sleeping, Sofija is dreaming.

It's the spring of 1925.

★

Elma is still in the guest room crouched over her long letter.

We wanted to hear Kaktiņš in Monte Carlo, but it didn't end up happening. On Sunday we could get Pagliacci with Kaktiņš, but there were only terrible tickets available. We didn't take them because we thought he'd be singing again soon, but it turned out that he didn't perform for the whole rest of the week.

I liked Capri the best. When we arrived in the evening, the waves were large, but after that there were only small waves without whitecaps, and the sky was overcast. The town of Capri is very nice, and it was possible to feel completely relaxed there, because it was so quiet. Vehicles aren't allowed into the town centre and locals have to carry everything in, in fact, they carry it in on their heads. In the morning, the roosters wake you up early, and after that there are birds, I think sparrows. I didn't hear any songbirds though. We had a room with a balcony and a sea view where you could recline in your chair and sit in the sun. There were pretty wisterias, different kinds of roses, and big bushes of daisies blooming all around.

The large clock in the corner of the room strikes one. Time to go help Hele, the letter will have to be finished later.

Elma is already getting up, but then suddenly sits back down and adds one more paragraph to the letter:

But I forgot to mention one other thing about Paris. On our last afternoon, we went up to the top of Eiffel Tower. The weather was pretty warm and overcast, there wasn't any wind, and so from up the top we didn't see much, because there was fog covering the entire city. The ride up is very comfortable, but even so when I looked down from the top platform I had this unpleasant feeling moving up my legs. Tingling and shivers running down. After a little while I got used to it, but my feet were still clammy with sweat. I was standing by myself on the top platform. Ansis had walked over to the other side, from there you couldn't see the ground at all, and for a second the most incredible fear came over me. I couldn't even remember where or who I was. But then Ansis came back and we rode down again together happily.

Notes

1. Latvian: light

2. Pēteris Stučka (1865-1932) was the head of the government of the Latvian Socialist Soviet Republic, a short-lived Bolshevik-backed state, which existed between 1918 and 1920 on the territory of present-day Latvia during the Latvian War of Independence prior to the victory of the Latvian Provisional Government.

3. German: Leave it!

4. The cabaret 'Piccadilly', restaurant 'Trocadero', and night club 'Foxtrott-Diele' were major destinations for Riga night life during this period.

5. The name of a newspaper: *The Newest News*

6. German: trash

7. Historic German name for Tallinn.

8. German: One moment, please!

9. Karl Tõnisson (1883-1962), also known as Brother Vahindra or Kārlis Tennisons, was Estonian by ethnicity but Latvian by citizenship and was the first person to teach Buddhism or declare themselves a Buddhist in the Baltic countries. He organised Latvia's first Buddhist congregation in Riga in 1924.

The Night Shift

Pauls Bankovskis

Translated by Mārta Ziemelis

NO ONE COULD AGREE on what happened in there. Each of them had their own version of events, their own opinion. Every imagined scene was more horrifying than the last.

'You burn in there, surrounded by fire, but you're never consumed,' said Zinaida. 'They're like the flames of Hell, only much hotter. Imagine the feeling of holding your hand in fire for a moment; only fire's all around you. It's much, much hotter than normal fire. Heat isn't just around you, but inside you too. Everything in your body boils, but doesn't change into coal or ash. You burn forever! That's God's purpose for sure; it's His punishment for our sins. I know if it happens to me, I'll have earned the punishment.'

These couldn't really be called testimonies. This group of people talked about things they hadn't experienced themselves. The things they said were stories that had been retold countless times, tossed back and forth and pondered repeatedly. They were guesses, based on personal experience, ideas or biases.

'I've sinned so, so much in my life,' said Zinaida. That was probably true. Still, she waved her traffic control wand with such initiative that it seemed like even this simple responsibility had become a ritual of repentence, penance and purification, constantly improved.

Mārtiņš was different. He was one of the leading supporters of theories to do with aliens.

'They hold you completely motionless,' Mārtiņš explained, 'but keep you conscious. They don't use any painkillers. Sometimes they put substances into your circulatory system that increase or cause pain. And then they do experiments, collect various samples.'

When Mārtiņš talked about aliens, he usually got carried away, stammered a bit, and fumbled nervously with his always-dirty glasses.

'They're especially interested in our reproductive system. That's why they insert various probes and measuring instruments into all the openings that they think have something to do with it.'

Every time Mārtiņš got to the openings and measuring instruments, he stared so hard at the person he was talking to that he began to look like a threatening probe himself.

I forgot to tell you how I came to join them. My bad luck started at about the same time as everyone else's. The financial crisis of 2009 was in full swing, but I only noticed it when it was too late. For some stupid reason, I'd taken out a loan and bought an apartment that I hoped to sell for more than I'd paid. There was a year and a half left on my car lease too. The stream of orders for brochures and posters, which had been consistent until then, suddenly dried up. The world was full of unskilled computer graphics artists and layout designers like me. I must admit, there was also my rather innocuous passion for gambling machines and beer. I had to start borrowing money, then selling this and that so I could repay my debts, then borrowing again, and so on. I didn't have rich relatives who could help. I didn't have many friends or acquaintances either. The few I did have were struggling along like naked men running through nettles, or had suddenly just died, one after the other.

So here I am – a ticket collector on public transportation. Honestly, I'm happy to at least have a job. I can't go back to working on a computer, if only because I don't have a computer anymore.

I should say straight off that I had no idea the main danger facing ticket collectors came from something other than drunk or aggressive fare dodgers. As it turns out, something completely different made my colleagues permanently nervous and irritable.

During my first days at work, I started to wonder if something in a ticket collector's job wasn't quite what it seemed to a passenger or pedestrian. One day, after Zinaida waved her traffic control wand and the bus stopped, opening its door, none of the ticket collectors wanted to get on first. Mārtiņš, Gennadiy, Juļa and all the rest hesitated; I was always the one who boarded the bus first. In the beginning, I told myself it was just my imagination, but I soon worked out that if I wasn't the first one on the bus, the other ticket collectors stood by the open door and watched me casually. Not just my co-workers, but the officers from the municipal police too. 'He doesn't know yet,' I once heard them whisper, and felt sure they were talking about me.

The secret was only revealed a few months later, when Laura – a sturdy woman, who looked a lot older than her age – joined our team. Now everyone sneakily tried to make it so that the first one to board the arriving vehicles would be her.

It was drizzling. We smoked, crowded together.

'It's time you knew,' said the mustachioed Gennadiy. 'Remember, we know about it, a few people from the municipal police do, but nobody else can know. Not even Laura, for now. Because no one would believe it. Now, have you heard of the blue bus?'

I nodded, surprised, unable to take Gennadiy's words and grave tone seriously. Of course, I'd heard of it, growing up. It was an urban legend about a blue bus that kidnapped children and took them away to the forest, never to be seen again. I read once, somewhere on the internet, that the story was most likely based on the massacre of Riga's Jews in Rumbula Forest in 1941. Jewish citizens were taken to the forest in bluish-grey transit buses.

'It looks the same as the others; all buses are blue now. It even looks as if there are passengers sitting inside, and a real driver at the wheel. People only realise it's not a normal bus when it's already too late. The door slams shut and the bus drives away.' Gennadiy went quiet.

Everyone stared at me.

'And after?' I asked.

'There is no after,' said Mārtiņš. 'No one taken away by the blue bus has ever been seen again. No one, not a single thing has been found – not even bones, or our green uniform vests. When it began people didn't understand, nobody was careful, whole teams boarded buses right away. Sometimes dozens of people disappeared in a week.'

'What about the bus itself?' I asked. 'It's got to be somewhere.'

'*Vot*,[1] that's the thing,' Gennadiy gestured, 'it should be somewhere, but it's not! Do you think we haven't searched? Do you think we haven't combed through all the bus garages, junkyards and scrap metal yards many times? Nothing! There's no such bus. Looking for it by route or by registration number is also hopeless. By day, it can be the No. 22 bus, but by night the No. 3 or No. 50 bus. Its registration number never matches up with any of the buses actually in use.'

'Do only ticket collectors disappear on it, or regular people from bus stops too?'

'We don't know for sure, but it seems like it leaves regular people alone,' said tall Juris. 'Since, if it didn't, could

114

it really stay a secret for so long, and would we really be the only ones to know about it?'

'But what about Rīgas satiksme?'[2] I asked. 'Surely the bus company knows something? Their employees are the ones disappearing! What do the families of the missing think?'

'Even if they do know, their lips are sealed,' Gennadiy dismissed the idea. 'If they know, obviously they'll never admit it. There's no point in talking to them. What sane person would believe in something like this? That's why, even if you know, it's easy to pretend you don't believe, that that kind of thing is impossible. All the traces have to be hidden, so that no one suspects the disappearances have anything to do with our work. Do you know how many people have already gone missing this year? Twenty-five!'

'There's even a theory,' Mārtiņš began in a half-whisper, 'that the bus isn't a bus, but a —'

'I don't believe it, I just don't believe it!' Zinaida interrupted him.

'Zinaida, let me finish,' Mārtiņš adjusted his glasses. 'There's a theory that this bus isn't actually a bus, but a shapeshifter.'

I guess I looked pretty stunned, judging by Mārtiņš' reaction. Mārtiņš, in the voice of a teacher worn out by an apathetic student, explained:

'It's some kind of living organism unknown until now, a life-form that changes its shape, so it can feed, and then returns to a state of hibernation, much like some animals sleep through the winter. According to this theory, the bus, or, more precisely, the bus-shaped organism, feeds on our disappeared colleagues. That might explain the cycles of the bus's appearances — maybe the bus, like a reptile, needs time to digest its victims... It could be that the bus is some unusual plant, a mutation, one of those insect-eaters. Have you seen *Little Shop of Horrors*? And then there are those freaky plants at the Yale University library, in the so-called Voynich[3] manuscript there, which nobody has been able to figure out to this day...' Mārtiņš's voice faded, and his eyes fixed on something invisible.

The bus came into view around the corner. From a distance, I tried to spot any suspicious signs – something unusual, different. I'd probably have felt a strange relief if I'd seen them. But the most terrifying thing was that there were no special signs. And that apparently a very ordinary bus can cause fear and disturbing uncertainty.

Zinaida raised her traffic control wand and the bus stopped by the side of the street with a heavy sigh. With a hiss, its doors opened. The inside looked like a regular transit bus; we could even see passengers. They were looking at us, some cranky, some nervous. I didn't rush to get on first; like the rest of my colleagues, I watched Laura out of the corner of my eye.

She didn't even glance at us as she threw herself on board. Nothing happened. A few seconds later, we got on too.

Almost a whole week passed. The night shifts were especially depressing. In the dark everything looked stranger and more threatening than during the day. The almost completely empty buses, illuminated on the inside, filled with tired silhouettes like half-alive shadows. The strange shapes cast on the walls were hunched and elongated, like an unsettling reminder of anatomical aids from school displaying cross-sections of human digestive tracts.

If Laura wasn't nearby, we would debate our theories as to what happens to the people kidnapped by the bus. I'd more or less taken note of all my co-workers' theories. For Zinaida, everything was based in religious ideas. Mārtiņš supported the extraterrestrial-physiological camp. Gennadiy, as a veteran of the war in Afghanistan, believed atrocities and physical torture were at play. Juļa thought sexual abuse awaited her in the bus. Tall Juris thought the bus was a time-travel portal, and that all the disappeared were living in the far-off future or past. Viktors thought the bus was an organ-harvesting lab for some criminal organisation, but Leons was convinced that secret military experiments were behind it, and that the Latvian secret service and NATO were complicit. Only Laura, like me, had no theories.

But unlike us, it would soon fall to Laura to find out the truth. The problem was that she, like the others who were missing, had no chance to tell anybody about her discoveries.

It was early one Wednesday, and we were all a little tired, but Gennadiy and Juris were also clearly hungover. A fine, freezing cold rain, like a stabbing fog carried on the wind, added to the sullen mood. It was damp and stuffy on the buses; it smelled like social inequality. I didn't like weather like this, because my glasses always fogged up when I got on the bus. We mostly didn't talk, just exchanged a few blunt words now and then. We climbed on and off the bus as though mechanically taking part in a ritual – first Laura, the others a moment later. She still hadn't noticed anything suspicious in our behaviour. And she never would.

It was the No. 3 bus from Bolderāja. As soon as Laura got on, the doors snapped shut with a hiss. Gennadiy almost got trapped inside, the hangover had made him less alert. With a pissed-off 'Aargh!', he twisted backwards and managed to kick the side of the bus. I think I mentioned – Laura was a sturdy woman. Wedged behind the other side of the bus door, she wasn't ready to give up yet. At first angry, then more desperate banging on the door came from inside. We suddenly couldn't make out what was happening – an opaque blackness had stretched out and covered the interior bus windows. Vomiting a puff of black diesel smoke into the wet, cold air, the bus drove off and ran a yellow light through the intersection. For a while we could still hear Laura's screams.

'*Ņihuja sebe!*'[4] said Gennadiy.

We were quiet. It was clear right away that the shift was now over. No one was even thinking of working anymore. All of us went to the bar, no questions asked. For Gennadiy and Juris, of course, it was a case of having a hair of the dog. We all drank the first brandy quickly, then another, and one more for good measure. Only then did I notice that my colleagues were giving me sideways looks.

'There it is,' said Juris. 'You're the newbie again. You'll have to get on first.'

Silence fell. The TV on the wall was showing the morning news with the sound off.

'But,' I faltered, 'I know everything now.'

'That doesn't matter,' said Mārtiņš. 'Even if you do know, you're the newbie and will have to get on first. Until someone else starts working here.'

Something in this logic suddenly no longer seemed fair to me.

'But only the very newest people get swallowed... disappear. Maybe sometimes the people who come right after them, but all of you are in almost no danger! You for example, Mārtiņš – which spot in line is yours?'

'I'm third. Zinaida and Juris came before me, but that doesn't matter. I've been fifth too. It's not as if people are waiting in line to grab this job.'

'Don't worry, mate,' Gennadiy tried to reassure me. 'Now at least a month will go by – or almost a month. It doesn't usually come back before that.'

'Yes, a month,' Mārtiņš nodded. 'There's even a theory that its appearances have something to do with the phases of the moon, like the tide...'

'I don't believe it, I just don't believe it!' Zinaida was already very drunk.

'Say, do you have any ideas about what happens in there?'

Mārtiņš leaned closer to me.

'Yes, well, no.' I got confused and remembered Laura's screams. 'Honestly, I don't have any ideas.'

'Oh, what difference does it make?' Gennadiy called to the bartender to pour everyone another round. 'Each of us has come up with a theory, but no one knows the truth.'

'We don't know, but we believe,' objected Zinaida.

'It's not a question of faith,' Mārtiņš said in a critical tone.

'Let's drink,' urged Gennadiy. 'To luck!'

The fact that I now knew what I was in danger from made getting on the bus both harder and, in a way, easier. Of course I was scared, horribly scared. But at least I wasn't tormented by suspicion toward my co-workers' intent, or guesswork about their incomprehensible behaviour waiting for me to get on the bus first. We didn't discuss the order anymore. We understood each other without words: I jumped on first, without hesitation, they followed. Nothing special happened, just the daily routine, made up of run-ins with the fare dodgers we caught, listening to colourful swearing and curses, tussles with drunk passengers and municipal police officers, and other things like that.

I'd taught myself not to think about what might happen if the bus doors suddenly slammed shut behind me and I got stuck inside. We usually don't think too often about the way things were before we came into the world, or what will happen when we're not here anymore. Yes, I know there are people who believe in life after death and things like that – people like our Zinaida. I've never been religious, though. My worldview is built on a pretty rational foundation; Paradise, Hell and Purgatory don't really have a place in it. The threat posed by one of these buses contradicted my world view, yet I tried to comfort myself with the thought that even this had some understandable explanation rooted in the laws of nature. The only thing that wouldn't leave me alone was the sound of Laura's screams.

Hunches and intuition have little to do with rational thinking. Still, I calmed myself with the thought that when my bus and my turn came, in some mysterious way I'd feel it and know. Since for the time being, I hadn't sensed anything special or different from the other times an ordinary bus stopped at the side of the street; I thought I was in no danger.

I think I mentioned that it was a lot harder to keep a cool head during night shifts. Darkness, tiredness and late-night passengers were a suitable backdrop for thoughts of my uncertain future and the possible horrors that were waiting for me. Would I really spend the rest of my life like this – working as a ticket collector on public transport? Was it even worth it to fear one day getting on a bus that I wouldn't be able to get off?

Soldiers often say that you never hear the bullet that kills you. I heard my bus, though. It was a few minutes past midnight. A night bus without a number. Saying I heard it wouldn't really be accurate, though, because my ears only picked up on the fact that it was moving soundlessly. Suddenly the city noises had fallen silent too – gulls weren't screeching at each other anymore, trains weren't rattling on the bridge, cars weren't rushing past, drunks weren't yelling in Old Riga. The bus was getting closer, crossing the tram tracks, swaying slowly. Zinaida raised her traffic control wand. A childish thought sprang to mind: I should delay her, take the wand away, not let her stop the bus, and so interfere with the course of my fate. But it was already too late. The bus had stopped and opened its doors. On the inside, it was no different from another bus; about a dozen passengers were sitting there. I hesitated to get on all the same. I suppose I'd been standing there for a while, because I heard Mārtiņš's 'Ahem' next to me.

I looked at my co-workers and realised from their eyes that they also knew. Gennadiy pursed his lips and shook his head sadly. Zinaida even waved at me briefly. I took a deep breath and climbed on.

Notes

1. Russian for, in this context, 'There you go' – a phrase used for emphasis.
2. Rīgas Satiksme is the public transportation company of the city of Riga.
3. The Voynich manuscript is an illustrated codex hand-written in an unknown writing system, the vellum of which has been carbon-dated to the early 15th century. Named after Wilfrid Voynich, the Polish book dealer who purchased it in 1912, it has been studied by many professional and amateur cryptographers, including American and British codebreakers from both World War I and World War II. No one has yet demonstrably deciphered the text, making it a famous case in the history of cryptography.
4. Vulgar Russian expression of surprise or amazement.

About the Authors

Writer and journalist **Pauls Bankovskis** (born 1973) was born in Līgatne, Latvia. He studied glass art at the Riga School for Applied Arts and Philosophy at the University of Latvia (1992–1996). His prose was first published in 1993. A prolific author, he has now published ten novels, several collections of short stories, books and works of non-fiction, and film scripts. In 2007 Pauls Bankovskis published his first children's book, *The Tiny-Noggins' Play House,* which was awarded the International Jānis Baltvilks Prize. Bankovskis' works have been translated into German, Czech, Finnish and English. His latest novel, *18,* was published within a series of historical novels entitled *We. Latvia. The 20th Century.*

Ilze Jansone (born 1982) is a Latvian writer and theologian. Jansone studied at the University of Latvia in the Faculty of Theology. She is best known for the short story 'Behind The Glass' (2006), her novels *Insomnia* (2010) and *The Only One* (2015), the collection of stories *Umurkums or Goodbye Feminism* (2013). Since 2013, Jansone has participated in the creation of a collection of articles *Construction Of Gender,* and compiled a collection of essays entitled *Nation Chronicles* (together with D. Hanovs and P. Daija).

Arno Jundze (born 1965) is a Latvian prose writer, cultural journalist, literary critic and theorist. He has hosted *100g of Culture* and other TV programmes, and is one of the creators of *Black on White* for Latvian television (LTV1). Jundze is an editor of the cultural news section for one of Latvia's biggest newspapers. Currently Jundze is head of the Latvian Writers' Union. He has also written two books for children and a novel, *Dust in an Hourglass*. His latest fantasy novel is *Christopher and the Order of Shadows*. Jundze's works for children have been nominated for the prestigious Jānis Baltvilks Award.

Sven Kuzmins (born 1985) is a Latvian writer, artist and actor. He mainly writes prose fiction and critical articles, but also experiments with various forms of visual arts and literature. He is known to the wider public as one of the initiators and authors behind the NERTEN sketch theatre project. He also hosts a weekly literary show on Latvian Radio 1. *Urban Shamans* is Kuzmins' first collection of stories, accompanied by his own graphic drawings. His works have been translated into English, Russian, Spanish, and Lithuanian, and published in various printed and online platforms. He is currently working on his second book.

Vilis Lācītis (real name Aleksandrs Ruģēns, born 1975) is a Latvian writer and musician. From 2002 to 2007 he played in the group Pupociklu Vasara. He then moved to the UK and studied anthropology at Oxford University. He became well-known for his writing in 2010, when his debut novel *Stroika to London* was published, about the life of Latvian migrant workers in England. The novel was signed with a pseudonym Vilis Lācītis; the author publicly appeared, dressed in a bear's mask, and his real name was not initially disclosed. The novel won a special prize at the Annual Literary Awards 2010 and was also nominated in the Best Debut category. This was followed by *To Ramen Lacples* (2011), which was originally created as a play, *The Long Way to Hantimansiysk* (2012, together with Schmidz Klonatan Wawert) and *The Amsterdam Principle* (2013). In January 2017, the English version of his first novel was published as *Stroika with a London View*.

ABOUT THE AUTHORS

Andra Neiburga (born 1957) is a prose writer and a well-known author of short stories. A graduate of the Latvian Academy of Art, she has worked as a designer for the magazines Avots and Karogs and has chaired the Latvian Young Writers' Association. Her first two highly acclaimed books were the short story collection *Stuffed Birds and Caged Birds*, and the children's book *The Story of Tille and the Dog Man* (1991). After these books, she only started publishing her work again in 2002. *Push, Push* is her latest collection of stories and has won her critical and public acclaim. Her stories have been turned into plays and staged in the New Riga Theatre. Several of her stories have been translated into English, French, German, Russian, Ukrainian and Lithuanian and published in anthologies abroad.

Author and art scholar **Gundega Repše** (born 1960) is a writer of prose, an essayist and critic. Repše has worked as an editor and contributor in various magazines and other media. Her prose has been published since 1979. Repše has published many novels; several of her works have been adapted for theatre. Her trilogy *Heavy Metal* is informed by autobiographical material and has become one of the most important works of contemporary Latvian literature. Repše's short story 'How Important Is It To Be Ernest' was included in the prose anthology *Dalkey Arhive Best European Fiction 2013*. The novel *Bogene* was published in 2016 as part of the *We. Latvia. The 20th Century* novel series. Repše's prose has been translated into English, German, French, Swedish, Russian, and other languages. Gundega Repše is a member of the Latvian Writers' Union and the Latvian PEN club. In 2000, she received the Annual Latvian Literature Award for her novel *Thumbelina*.

Dace Rukšāne-Ščipčinska (born 1969) is a Latvian writer and journalist. After finishing high school she studied

Medicine and Biology and additionally participated in the SOURCES 2 Script Development Workshop in Vienna. Rukšāne became well-known in 2002 for her novel *The Little Affair* (Romāniņš) that touched upon the subjects of feminine sexuality. It was followed by *Bedtime Stories of Beatrice*, and *Why were you Crying?*, as well as several articles devoted to intimate subject matters and relationships. During the 1990s Rukšāne wrote poetry, and in the early 2000s several of her plays were staged in various theatres in Latvia. Her novels have been published in Germany and Denmark. In 2002, Rukšāne became a regular contributor to a weekly column in *Sestdiena* magazine. From 2004 until 2012 she was editor-in-chief of *Lilit* magazine.

Film director and writer **Kristīne Želve** was born in 1970. She studied film directing and cultural management at the Academy of Culture of Latvia. She has made several documentary films and video works. She is contributor to various Latvian media outlets and also runs a culture broadcast on Latvian Television. Her first book, a collection of short stories entitled *The Girl Who Cut My Hair* was published in 2011. The author was awarded the Annual Prize for Literature and the Annual Prize for Culture of the daily newspaper *Diena*.

Juris Zvirgzdiņš (born 1941) is known for being one of the most productive writers of highly esteemed literature, having written more than twenty books for children. His works have received many awards, and have been translated into several languages. Eleven radio plays have been staged of his works. He is known namely for his educational books which are dearly loved by children. His book *Muffa: Story of the White Baby Rhinoceros* was included in the prestigious White Ravens Catalogue in 2012.

About the Translators

Kaija Straumanis translates from German and Latvian, and holds an MA in Literary Translation Studies from the University of Rochester. Her translations include works by Latvian authors Inga Ābele, Zigmunds Skujiņš, Jānis Joņevs, Egīls Venters and Inga Žolude, among others. She is also the editorial director for Open Letter Books.

Suzanne McQuade is a translator, writer, editor, and photographer living in Cincinnati, Ohio. She learned Latvian in 1994 as an exchange student in Riga, and began translating Latvian fiction over subsequent years as a means of maintaining her connection to both the language and the culture of Latvia. She is the translator of Inga Žolude's novel *Warm Earth* as well as Žolude's award-winning collection of short stories, *A Solace For Adam's Tree*.

Uldis Balodis grew up in Arizona, a descendant of the World War II Latvian refugee community in the United States, and is a native speaker of Latvian and English. He has studied over 30 languages, including Navajo, Sanskrit, and Sámi. He holds a Ph.D. in linguistics and has a particular interest in endangered and less spoken languages. As a translator, he has worked with a variety of literary genres, both fiction and non-fiction. His translation of Zigmunds Skujiņš' novel *Nakedness* will be published by Vagabond Voices in the UK in 2018 as well as *Trillium* for which he was a contributing translator and which will be the first ever poetry anthology in English and Livonian, an endangered Finnic language native to Latvia.

ABOUT THE TRANSLATORS

Ieva Lešinska (born 1958) is a writer, journalist and translator living and working in Riga, Latvia, after many years spent studying and working in the United States, Sweden and Germany. Her translations of Latvian poetry and fiction into English have been published both in the UK and the USA, as well as in electronic media. Well known for her many Latvian translations of Anglo-American poetry, fiction and documentary prose, she has also published many interviews, essays and book reviews.

Mārta Ziemelis studied Italian at the University of Toronto. She has been a French-English translator for several years, and is currently working as a Latvian-English translator. Her published translations include 'Do you exist, or did my mind invent you?', a piece by Latvian poet Gunta Micāne, as well as *The Water of Life*, a novel by French-Canadian author Daniel Marchildon. She is currently working on a number of Latvian-English translations, and is honoured to have her work included in *The Book of Riga*.

Žanete Vēvere Pasqualini was born in Riga. She graduated from the Faculty of Foreign Languages, University of Latvia, in 1995, at the same time completing a course in Italian language and culture at the University of Perugia. Žanete is fluent in English, Italian and Russian and also has basic knowledge of French. She worked for the Latvian Embassy in Rome which has led to her now dividing her time between Latvia and Italy. Žanete has translated literature for both adults and children. In 2016 her translation from Italian to Latvian, 'Pagrīdes iecelotāji' by Valentina Paravano and Valerio Tassara, was published by Pētergailis, as was a collection of children's poetry, *The Noisy Classroom,* by Ieva Flamingo.